# TERRIBLE
# TRACTORS
# OF
# TEXAS

## Here's what readers from around the country are saying about Johnathan Rand's *AMERICAN CHILLERS:*

" I think these books are awesome!"
*-Marcus L., age 11, Michigan*

"I just finished THE MICHIGAN MONSTERS!
It was the best book I've ever read!"
*-Stacey G., age 9, Florida*

"Johnathan Rand's books are my favorite.
They're really creepy and scary!"
*-Jeremy J., age 9, Illinois*

"My whole class loves your books! I have two
of them and they are really, really cool."
*-Katie R., age 12, California*

"I never liked to read before, but now I read
all the time! The 'Chillers' series is great!"
*-Lauren B., age 10, Ohio*

"I love AMERICAN CHILLERS because they
are scary, but not too scary, because I don't want
to have nightmares."
*-Adrian P., age 11, Maine*

"I loved it when Johnathan Rand came to our
school. He was really funny. His books are great."
*-Jennifer W., age 8, Michigan*

# Don't miss these exciting, action-packed books by Johnathan Rand:

## Michigan Chillers:

#1: Mayhem on Mackinac Island
#2: Terror Stalks Traverse City
#3: Poltergeists of Petoskey
#4: Aliens Attack Alpena
#5: Gargoyles of Gaylord
#6: Strange Spirits of St. Ignace
#7: Kreepy Klowns of Kalamazoo
#8: Dinosaurs Destroy Detroit
#9: Sinister Spiders of Saginaw
#10: Mackinaw City Mummies

## American Chillers:

#1: The Michigan Mega-Monsters
#2: Ogres of Ohio
#3: Florida Fog Phantoms
#4: New York Ninjas
#5: Terrible Tractors of Texas
#6: Invisible Iguanas of Illinois
#7: Wisconsin Werewolves
#8: Minnesota Mall Mannequins
#9: Iron Insects Invade Indiana
#10: Missouri Madhouse
#11: Poisonous Pythons Paralyze Pennsylvania
#12: Dangerous Dolls of Delaware
#13: Virtual Vampires of Vermont

## Adventure Club series:

#1: Ghost in the Graveyard
#2: Ghost in the Grand

# www.americanchillers.com

AudioCraft Publishing, Inc.
PO Box 281
Topinabee Island, MI 49791

# #5: Terrible Tractors of Texas

## Johnathan Rand

# An AudioCraft Publishing, Inc. book

Graphics layout/design consultant: Chuck Beard, Straits Area Printing

Book warehouse and storage facilities provided by Clarence and Dorienne's Storage, Car Rental & Shuttle Service, Topinabee Island, MI. Warehouse security provided by Abby, Salty, and Lily Munster.

Paperback ISBN 1-893699-28-5
Hardcover ISBN 1-893699-29-3

Printed in USA

Third Printing, June 2004

# Terrible
# Tractors
# of
# Texas

Visit the official 'American Chillers' web
site at:

www.americanchillers.com

Featuring excerpts from upcoming stories, interviews,
contests, official American Chillers wearables, and *more!*
Plus, join the American Chillers fan club!

# 1

*"Jake! It's five-thirty! Get a move on!"*

I groaned. Dad was yelling from outside, and he knew I wasn't out of bed yet. I'm usually up by five in the morning to begin my chores around the farm. Today, however, I was really tired, and I'd fallen back to sleep.

I groaned again, and climbed out of bed.

*Might as well get started*, I thought.

The roosters were already crowing, and I could hear the hens clucking near the barn. Our family has a small ranch about a hundred miles from Dallas, Texas. We have chickens, horses, hogs, cows . . . the

11

usual farm animals. I wouldn't trade it for the world, but sometimes, the work can be pretty boring.

Today, however, would be different. My best friend, John Culver, was coming. He used to be my neighbor when we lived in Houston, but we moved away to the farm a couple of years ago. I don't get to see him much anymore.

But today he would be coming to spend the whole *week* with us! John is eleven, the same age as me. We have always gotten along great, and we like a lot of the same things.

And it was July. The middle of summer vacation. School wouldn't be starting for another two months!

Not that I don't like school, because I do. It's just that summer in Texas is so much *fun*.

With John visiting, the coming week was going to be nothing but fun with a capital 'F'.

At least, that's what I thought when I got up that morning. I thought that we'd spend the coming days fishing and swimming and biking.

That wasn't what would happen. Oh, we would have fun for a little while.

But by tonight, everything would change—and our fun would be over.

Our fun would be over . . . and the terror would begin.

# 2

I ate a quick bowl of corn flakes before heading outside. The sun was already coming up, and the eastern sky was all pink and yellow. If you ever come to Texas, don't miss the sunrises. We have some of the coolest sunrises in the world. The sunsets are beautiful, too.

It took me a couple of hours to take care of the animals. We have hired hands that help out, but it's always been my job to look after the livestock. It's hard work, and I'm not complaining.

It's just that I *really* wanted to get everything done before John got here. That way we would have all day to hang out. We could go down to the creek and fish, catch turtles and frogs . . . heck, we would have a *blast.*

I went into the barn to find more food for the geese. We have seven geese on the farm and when they don't get fed on time, they get really cranky. When they saw me coming this morning, they started honking and making all kinds of noise.

In the barn, we have several big pieces of farm equipment, including some really cool tractors. They're awesome! Dad used to take me for rides when I was little, but now I can operate them all by myself. One of the tractors—a big red one—is one that I drive a lot. It's my favorite.

There is some other heavy machinery we have, too. Dad bought a bulldozer and a small crane at an auction, but they're too big to put in the barn. When they're not being used, we keep them out back near the corral.

"Jake!" I heard Dad call out. I turned and walked out of the barn.

Dad was standing by a big green diesel storage tank. Most of the tractors and farm equipment run on diesel.

"Yeah?" I replied, squinting in the morning sun.

"I'm going into Dallas today. I'll need you to fuel up all of the equipment for the workers. I want to use the new fuel in everything to see how it works.

*Shoot,* I thought. Fueling up all of the equipment would take another hour. Dad bought this new experimental gas that is supposed to make the equipment run longer.

I had my doubts. Fuel is fuel. It wasn't going to make any difference.

I was wrong.

*Really* wrong.

The gas . . . the new experimental fuel that Dad wanted to try out in all the farm equipment . . . would do more than simply make the equipment run longer.

A *lot* more.

And when I fueled up all of the tractors and dozers and equipment with that gas, I had no way of knowing the trouble we were in for.

"Okay," I answered, and I turned and walked back into the barn.

*Gas up everything?!?!* I thought. *There is no way I'll finish before John gets here!*

By now, the geese were really making an awful lot of racket. They were hungry.

I had just walked out the front of the barn when I spotted something that made me freeze in my tracks. I didn't move, for I knew better.

And if you saw what I saw, you'd do the exact same thing.

Right next to my foot, only inches away, was a rattlesnake.

A *big* one.

*And he was coiled up, preparing to strike!*

# 3

I didn't move a single muscle. That's the only thing you can do when you're confronted with a rattlesnake. I wear thick leather boots when I work, but that doesn't mean that a rattlesnake can't bite through them.

And if this one did, I'd be in *serious* trouble.

So, I froze like an ice cube.

The snake remained poised, ready to attack and sink its razor-sharp fangs into my leg.

And then:

*Giggling.* I heard giggling coming from the side of the barn!

I still hadn't moved an inch, but now I slowly turned my head to see who was laughing.

"Haha! Gotcha!" a voice exclaimed.

*John!*

I relaxed, and took a step back from the snake. Obviously it was fake, but it sure was a *good* fake! It really looked like an actual, coiled rattler!

"Isn't that cool?" John said.

"That's awesome!" I replied.

"It's yours. I bought it at a store for you. I have one, too, and I fool *everybody* with it!"

"For me?!?!" I exclaimed. "Gosh . . . thanks!"

I picked up the fake snake and looked at him.

"When did you get here?" I asked.

"Just a few minutes ago. Our car is in the driveway on the other side of your house. My mom and dad are inside, talking to your mom and dad."

"Help me finish up, and we'll head down to the creek," I said. "I'm almost done. We just have to gas up the equipment."

"Cool!"

I put the coiled snake on a fencepost, and we got to work. With John's help, it didn't take long to finish up with the livestock.

Then it was time to fuel up the equipment. I drove the tractors out of the barn and up to the tank filled with the experimental fuel. That didn't take too long, either. After filling each tractor, I drove them back into the barn.

However, since I'm not allowed to drive the heavy equipment out back, Dad would have to fill those up himself. I wish I could, but Dad says not for a few more years.

"This gas smells funny," John said as we filled up the last piece of equipment. "It smells like rotten bananas."

"It's some kind of experimental gas that Dad wants to try out. He says it's supposed to be better than the diesel fuel we normally use."

"It stinks," he said, holding his nose.

Just then, I heard shouting. A *girl* shouting. And she wasn't very far away.

I turned, puzzled by the noise. I don't have any brothers or sisters.

"That's the bad news," John said dryly. "My little sister is going to stay here all week, too."

*Oh no! Janey is a whiney little brat!*

"You're kidding?!?!" I said.

John shook his head. "I wish I was," he replied. "But Mom asked her if she wanted to stay, and she said yes. She's never been to a farm before. Your parents said that it was okay, too. So . . . we're stuck with her."

What a drag. Janey is a pest. She'd want to tag

along with us everywhere we go!

Then I had an idea.

"Let's hide from her!" I hissed. "Maybe we can sneak off down to the creek without her!"

"Good thinking!" John agreed.

I finished filling up the dozer and wiped my hands on a rag. I could hear Janey calling out, trying to find us.

However, we were behind the barn and she was in front. She couldn't see us!

John peered around the corner.

"Can you see her?" I asked.

"She just went into the barn," John replied.

"Cool! Let's make a run for it! She'll never find us!"

We darted around a crane and ran along the corral . . . but we didn't get very far.

Suddenly, Janey began screaming. Not a fake, girly scream . . . *but a scream of all-out terror!*

# 4

Janey's screams were awful. Whatever was going on was *serious*.

John and I stopped, and our feet kicked up a cloud of dust. We immediately spun and began running around to the front of the barn.

"She's never screamed like that before!" John huffed as we raced to help.

"She sounds like she's really hurt!" I said.

We darted around the corner of the barn and raced inside. Janey's screams of terror continued.

*"Over there!"* I cried. *"She's over there! On the other side of the tractors!"*

I knew that something had to be horribly, horribly wrong.

We sprinted past the equipment to find Janey flat against the back of the barn! She was scared stiff, and her eyes were bugging out of her head!

And right in front of her, two feet away, was the reason for her fear.

A goose.

A plain old, ordinary goose.

It honked a couple of times, pecked the ground, then honked some more.

"What's wrong?!?!" I shouted.

Janey was still shrieking like crazy, and I placed my hands over my ears.

*"The giant ducky is attacking me!"* Janey screeched. She had backed up against the wall, and she couldn't go any farther.

"For crying out loud," I said. "It's not a giant ducky! It's just a silly goose. He won't hurt you!"

"He attacked me!" Janey repeated. She was crying now, and she wouldn't budge one inch from the wall. "He's trying to eat me!"

"He didn't attack you," I said. "He just thinks that you have food for him. He's not going to eat you."

*"Remember . . . she's never been to a farm before,"* John whispered. *"Just be glad she didn't see a goat."*

I smiled, and walked up to the goose.

"Go on," I said, waving my hand at the bird. "Git! Get outside!"

The goose scooted beneath a tractor, clucking and honking.

"See?" John said. "It was only a goose. He's not going to hurt you."

"He had big teeth and he tried to bite me!"

I rolled my eyes.

"Geese don't have teeth," I insisted. "Come on, John."

As soon as John and I turned to leave, Janey unglued herself from the wall and began to follow.

"Huh-uh," John said, shaking his head. He stopped to face her. "You're not coming."

"Mom says I can."

"I say you can't."

"I'll tell Daddy."

"Daddy doesn't like you. He's going to swap you for a set of golf clubs."

"Is not!"

"Is too!"

"Is not!"

"Is too!"

This was going nowhere, fast.

"Enough!" I said loudly. "Janey . . . you can come with us . . . *if* you promise to leave us alone."

"I promise!" she said, bobbing her head.

"Come on, John," I said. The three of us walked past the parked tractors and out the door.

Suddenly, I stopped.

Something was wrong. There was something odd about one of the tractors.

"What?" John asked. "What's the matter?"

"I . . . I'm not sure," I replied.

My eyes scanned a few of the machines. There were several tractors and an old push lawn mower parked in a cluster, right where I'd left them. One of the tractors—the red one that I drive a lot—was parked near the door.

"This tractor," I said curiously. "It's . . . it's . . . ."

I paused. John and Janey were silent, waiting for me to finish.

*"Oh my gosh!"* I suddenly exclaimed. I leapt back, pulling John and Janey with me. *"This tractor! Look at it! It's . . . it's alive! It's coming to life! We have to get out of here!"*

# 5

Janey screamed.

John screamed.

I screamed, too. As loud as I could.

The three of us whirled and started to run.

*"It's coming!"* I shouted. *"It's right behind us!"*

Janey was in front of us and she ran like lightning, screaming her head off.

I slowed, and I grabbed John's arm. He slowed, too.

"Okay, okay," I laughed. "That's good enough."

John suddenly realized that I had only been playing a prank on Janey.

"It worked!" he exclaimed. "Man . . . you even had *me* going!"

"I owed you one for scaring me with the snake," I smirked.

"Well, you sure got me back. Janey, too!"

Janey had never looked back. She ran across the driveway, over the yard, and disappeared into the house, screaming all the way.

"That was kind of a mean trick," John said. Then he flashed a crooked grin. "I wish I'd thought of it!"

We gave each other a high-five.

"Now," I said, "we can go to the creek without being bugged by your little sister."

We set out across the field. The creek isn't far away, and it only took a few minutes to reach it.

Just like I'd planned, we spent the day catching turtles and frogs and lizards. I even caught a small fish with my bare hands!

After a few hours, we hiked back to the farm. Some of the workers were in the field, and a couple of them were tending to the horses in the corral.

"This is going to be a great week," John said. "I'm glad you invited me."

"No problem," I said, "as long as you don't mind helping with the morning chores."

"Are you kidding? This is going to be the best week of the summer! I love it here!"

And then I had an idea.

"Hey . . . I'll take you for a ride on one of the tractors. Dad doesn't let me drive the real big ones behind the barn, but we can take one of the smaller ones from inside."

"Yeah!" John replied. "I've never ridden on a tractor before. My dad has an old riding mower, but that's pretty boring."

"These tractors are cool," I said. "They're really powerful."

By this time, I'd completely forgotten about the experimental gas. After we'd fueled up the farm equipment, I never even gave it another thought.

Until we walked into the barn. That's when things got really freaky.

The day was hot, but a sudden cold chill swept through me.

John stopped in his tracks and gasped.

And we both knew that what we were seeing was no joke.

The red tractor . . . the one I drive most of the time . . . was moving . . . *all by itself!*

Not only was it moving by itself—*it was coming right at us!*

# 6

*"Holy smokes!"* I yelled! *"Let's get out of here!"*

Gravel flew as John and I whirled and fled. I had no idea what was going on, and I didn't want to. Seeing the red tractor moving all by itself was like some weird movie.

John and I ran, yelling and screaming, across the dirt driveway and over the yard. Mom heard our shrieks and she was already at the door. She was standing on the porch, holding the screen open—which was a good thing, too. We were running so fast, we would have never been able to stop in time.

*"What on earth is going on?!?!?!"* Mom demanded.

We flew past her, through the open door, and into the house. I almost fell over a chair!

*"The tractor!"* I said, gasping for breath. *"It's alive! It's moving all by itself!"*

Mom frowned and came back inside. The screen door banged closed.

"That was a very mean thing to do to Janey," Mom said. "She thought that the tractors really were after her!"

"Honest, Mrs. Sherwood!" John pleaded. "This time we're *serious!* Jake and I both saw it!"

I nodded in agreement. "It's true, Mom!" I said, pointing out the window. "Look! Right now!"

John and I ran to the living room window, and Mom turned.

"See!" John said, pointing. "It's moving! It's moving all by itself!"

The red tractor was already out the barn door, and was slowly crawling across the dirt driveway. Just watching it gave me the chills.

And then:

It stopped. The tractor sat motionless in the driveway.

John, Mom and I waited as tense seconds ticked by.

Suddenly, I spotted movement behind the tractor.

While we watched, one of Dad's hired hands emerged from behind the left rear tire.

"That tractor wasn't moving by itself," Mom said, walking away from the window. "One of the workers was pushing it."

I suddenly felt really silly. John and I had thought that the tractor was moving all by itself, which was impossible.

"Something must be wrong," I said. "Come on."

We left the house and walked across the yard to the driveway. A few geese waddled about, and some of the chickens were pecking at the ground near the barn. The workman was leaning over, staring at the tractor and scratching his head.

"What's wrong?" I asked.

He turned, looked at us, and shrugged.

"I don't rightly know," he said. "The bugger just won't start. I pushed it out here in the sun to have a look."

He climbed up into the seat and turned the key. The engine chugged and sputtered, but it wouldn't start.

"Come on," the worker said.

*Chug-a-chug-a-chug-a-chug.* The engine burped and hiccoughed, but that was it.

"Well, ain't that the darndest thing," the

workman said. He climbed out of the seat. "Come on, boys," he said. "Help me put 'er back in the barn."

John and I helped push the tractor. The workman thanked us.

"Guess I'll have to look at the motor after the weekend," he said. "See you kids later." And with that, he left the barn.

I smiled and shook my head.

"Looks like we got a little of our own medicine," I said. "I really thought that tractor was moving by itself."

"So did I," John replied. "We should have known. Tractors can't move by themselves."

John was wrong.

Tractors *can* move by themselves.

And at that very moment, all of them were getting ready.

They were getting ready—to take over.

By this time tomorrow, the tractors would be in charge.

The horrifying nightmare was about to begin.

# 7

John's mom and dad had left earlier that day, and the five of us—Mom, Dad, Janey, John, and me—had pork chops and corn on the cob for supper.

And then Dad gave us the bad news.

We were all seated around the table. Dad looked over at me.

"Your mother and I will be going to another auction tomorrow," he explained. "Janey is too young to be wandering around the ranch by herself. I want her to stay with you and John at all times."

My heart sank. John and I had planned on going back to the creek to catch frogs.

"And one more thing," Dad continued. "Since it's

Sunday, none of the hired hands will be coming in. There is a lot of work that needs to be done. It will take you most of the day."

My heart plummeted even more. Not only would Janey have to tag along all day . . . but John and I would have to spend the day working!

It just wasn't fair.

But there's one thing I've learned: don't even try to argue with Dad. When he's got his mind set on something, there's no use trying to change it.

"Okay," I muttered, trying to hide my disappointment.

*Well,* I thought. *At least we still have this evening. We could go back to the creek and fish for a while.*

And so, that's what we did. With Janey tagging along, we hiked back to the small stream and fished until it got dark. We caught a bunch of catfish before it was time to go. Surprisingly, Janey wasn't much of a pest at all. She sat on the bank of the creek and watched us fish.

By the time we made it back to the house, it was already dark. The sky was speckled with millions of stars, and the air was filled with the chiming of crickets. John and I sat on the porch and sipped lemonade, while Janey wandered across the driveway by the barn to catch fireflies.

"Don't go far," I warned her.

"I won't," she replied, and giggled happily as she skipped away.

John and I relaxed and talked about the fish we had caught, and made plans to go back to the creek. An owl hooted somewhere in the darkness, and I heard Janey giggle as she caught another firefly. Inside our house, I could hear the faint sound of the television.

That's one of the things I love about where I live. At night, everything is so calm and peaceful.

Well, it was calm and peaceful at the moment. At the moment, the Texas night was quiet and serene.

All of that was about to change—and it began when a tractor suddenly roared to life in the barn.

# 8

I was telling John about a big catfish that I caught last summer.

"You should have seen it!" I exclaimed. I sipped on my lemonade. "It was huge!"

"Did you take a—"

John was suddenly interrupted by the roar of a tractor starting. The noise startled both of us, and our gaze shot in the direction of the barn.

A light glowed from a post in the driveway, illuminating the yard, part of the corral, and the front of the barn.

"What's going on?" I said.

And then I had an awful thought. John had the

same thought, too, because both of us, at the same time, said:

"*Janey!*"

I set my lemonade on the porch and sprang. John was right behind me, and we tore across the yard. Gravel crunched beneath our feet as we sprinted across the driveway and approached the open barn doors.

There is a switch on the inside of the barn that turns on a single light that hangs from the rafters. It's the only light in the barn, but it's not very bright.

I clicked it on.

Janey was standing near the red tractor. The one that the hired hand had a problem with. Her back was to us, and she was staring up at the machine that towered above her.

Only now, there was no problem with the tractor at all—

*Because it was running!*

"*Janey!*" I shouted. "*What are you doing?!?!*"

Janey ignored me. She just kept staring up at the tractor.

I ran to the tractor, leapt into the seat, and turned the key. The motor died instantly.

"What did you think you were doing?!?!" I said, staring at Janey. I removed the key from the ignition and jumped to the ground.

"Why did you do that?" I asked her.

Janey shook her head.

"I didn't do it," was all she said.

"Janey . . . don't fib," John ordered. "Why did you start the tractor?"

Again, Janey shook her head. "I didn't," she insisted. "Cross my heart." She dragged a finger across her chest, making a big 'X'. "I chased a firebug in here, and the tractor started all by itself."

"It did not," John said. "You climbed up on it and turned the key. Tractors don't start all by themselves."

"This one did," she said, nodding her head. "And it blinked its eyes at me, too."

"Tractors don't have eyes, Janey," I said. "They have lights."

"He blinked his lights at me. I think he might be mad."

*For crying out loud,* I thought. *Janey is kooky.*

"You're lucky you weren't hurt," I said. "If you had put the tractor into gear by accident, you could have been in a lot of trouble."

I went around to all of the tractors and removed the keys from them. If Janey was going to wander around and play with the equipment, I wanted to be sure that she wouldn't hurt herself . . . or someone else, for that matter.

We left the barn and went inside. It was getting kind of late, and I knew Sunday morning was going to come early. John and I would have to be up at five to begin the day's chores. Plus, with Mom and Dad going to the auction, we'd be working a long day, that was for sure.

However, after I thought about it for a while, I realized that it probably wasn't going to be as bad as I expected. John is a really great friend, and he seemed happy to help out around the ranch. Maybe even a little excited about it.

And Janey. She hadn't been as pesky as I thought. Sure, starting the tractor wasn't a smart thing to do, but gosh . . . she's just a little kid. She probably didn't know any better.

We hit the sack. Janey slept in one of the guest bedrooms next to mine. I have a bunk bed, so John slept in my room on the top bunk, while I slept on the bottom bunk. I think I fell asleep as soon as I closed my eyes.

I opened them the moment I heard John's frantic whispering.

*"Jake! Jake! Wake up!"*

It was really dark, and I couldn't see a thing.

"*Jake! Wake up! A tractor is running in the barn!*"

I propped myself up on my elbows.

"Wh . . . what?" I stammered. I was still half-asleep.

"*There's a tractor running in the barn!*" John exclaimed.

I froze, listening intently.

*He was right! I could hear a motor running!*

But it wasn't possible!

It wasn't possible—*because I had taken all of the keys from the tractors!*

# 9

I threw off my covers and leapt out of bed. John scrambled down from the top bunk, and we both bolted to my open bedroom window.

My heart was pounding in my chest. I was wide awake now, and I listened to the roar of the tractor in the still, dark night.

And then:

It stopped.

The tractor sputtered and coughed. The engine stopped. The only thing we could hear were crickets. And a cow. I could hear one of our cows making a gentle *moooo* somewhere in the field.

But the tractor was silent.

After a few moments, John spoke again.

"How . . . how—"

"It's impossible," I interrupted. "I have all of the keys. All of them are on my dresser."

"Maybe a robber is trying to steal one!" John presumed. "Maybe there's a burglar out there!"

"No," I said. I strained my eyes to try and see through the darkness. The light over the driveway wasn't on, and the night was like a dark cloak. "A burglar isn't going to start a tractor and drive away with it. It would make too much noise."

We continued listening. The pulsating drone of crickets was almost overwhelming.

But that was all that we heard.

"Do you think we both could have dreamed it?" John asked.

"Huh-uh," I replied, shaking my head. "I heard a tractor. So did you."

"Well, it's not running now," John said.

We were silent for a moment, listening for any sounds. We could only hear crickets in the field. Even the wise old owl must have gone to bed.

"Well," I said. "We'll figure it out in the morning. There must be some reason why—"

Suddenly, two white eyes began to glow from the barn! They lit up the entire driveway!

John and I gasped.

*The lights of the tractor had turned on all by themselves!*

It wasn't possible, and I knew it. The lights couldn't be turned on without the keys.

I spun and bolted to my bedroom door and clicked on the light.

I stared at my dresser.

*The keys to all of the tractors were piled in a heap!*

I was scared, alright. You bet I was.

But suddenly, the tractor started up again . . .and I was more than just scared.

I was *horrified.*

# 10

There was no way a tractor can start itself.

*No way.*

There had to be some explanation for what was happening.

"Come on," I urged John. "We've got to go find out what's going on."

And so, the two of us, in our pajamas, slipped out of the house and into the yard. We could hear the tractor running, and we could see its lights were shining out the open barn door.

*How can this be?* I thought. *How can a tractor start all by itself? And turn on lights?*

It can't. It was as simple as that.

We walked, barefoot, across the yard.

But when we reached the driveway, the tractor motor suddenly stopped. The lights remained on for another moment, then blinked out.

John and I stopped and listened. We watched.

The light on the post above glowed, casting a haunting, bluish glow over the yard and across the front of the barn. Crickets chimed. Far away, a dog barked twice, then fell silent.

The open barn door was like a giant, black cave.

*"Do you think someone is in there?"* John asked.

*"No,"* I whispered back. *"I mean . . . I guess it's possible. But even if there was, there is no way they could start the tractor without the keys."*

We waited a few more minutes. Finally, I looked at John.

"Let's go," I said.

He must have misunderstood me, because he turned and began walking toward the house. I had already started off toward the barn.

*"Wait!"* he turned and whispered loudly. *"Where are you going?!?!"*

*"To the barn,"* I replied. *"That's what I meant when I said 'let's go'. We have to go find out what's going on."*

John walked quickly to where I was standing in the driveway, the two of us walked toward the dark barn door.   If anyone could have seen us, we probably looked pretty silly.   Two kids, wearing pajamas, tip-toeing across a dirt driveway in the middle of the night!

When we reached the barn, we stopped. Beyond the large, open door, inside the barn, I could make out the shadows and silhouettes of the heavy machinery.  They sat in the darkness like giant metal insects, waiting for their prey.

I stepped inside the barn, reached out, and found the light switch.  I flicked it on.

Nothing.

*The light didn't turn on!*

*"What's wrong?"* John whispered.

I flicked the switch a few more times.   Still nothing.

*"This is really weird,"* I thought.

As my eyes grew more accustomed to the dark, I could see more of the hulking forms of the tractors parked in the barn.  I walked over to the red one, the one that Janey had started earlier in the evening.

*"What are you looking for?"* John asked.

*"A key,"* I replied, climbing up onto the tractor. *"It can't start without a key."*

I reached out and fumbled around, and my hand finally found the ignition.

*No key.*

*Impossible,* I thought.

I climbed back down and stood next to the tractor, wondering how on earth it could have started all by itself. And how the lights had turned on.

No matter how hard I thought, I couldn't explain it.

"Well," I said to John, "we might as well just go back to bed and try and figure this out in the—"

I stopped speaking.

Behind us, there was a heavy squeaking sound. John and I spun, but we were too late.

Suddenly, the barn door slammed shut all by itself!

We were trapped in the barn—*in total darkness!*

# 11

I screamed. John screamed. We stumbled forward in the darkness. My hands found the door.

"Help!" I cried. "Help us! Mom! Dad!"

We pounded on the door with the palms of our hands.

"Please! Someone!" I shouted in the darkness. "Let us out of here!"

All of a sudden, the huge barn door swung open! I could see the dark shape of my dad . . . and he didn't look happy.

"What are you two doing out here?!?!" he demanded.

"I . . . uh . . . ." I stammered. I couldn't get the words out of my mouth.

"A tractor started up all by itself, Mr. Sherwood!" John blurted out. "It really, *really* did! We came out to see what was going on!"

"Tractors don't start themselves, John," my dad replied sternly. "You might be able to fool Janey, but not me."

"We're not making it up, Dad!" I pleaded. "We saw the tractor's lights on. We could hear it running. It was this one."

I turned and pointed at the red tractor.

"I think that's the one the worker was having trouble with," Dad said.

"Yeah," I replied. "He couldn't get it started. He said he was going to have a look at it on Monday."

"Well, then how did it start?" Dad asked. "Someone had to start it."

He glanced at me, then at John, then back to me. I could tell he didn't believe us.

"You didn't hear it running?" I asked.

Dad shook his head. "I was asleep, until I heard voices. I came out to see who was here. I had no idea you two were in the barn."

"You sure scared us when you closed the barn door," John said.

"I didn't know you were in there. Sorry about that. Now . . . you two go back to bed. You have a lot of work ahead of you in the morning."

Dad was right. We would have a lot of work ahead of us.

But it had nothing to do with chores around the house.

We would spend the day trying to stop vicious, bloodthirsty tractors and other machines.

Machines that came alive . . . all by themselves.

# 12

The roosters began to crow before my alarm went off. I woke up, sat up in bed, and took a deep breath. I could smell bacon and eggs and sausage.

*Today is going to be a long day,* I thought.

Of course, at the time, I had no idea just how long it would be.

John awoke, and the two of us stumbled sleepily into the kitchen. Mom had made a huge breakfast. It sure was a great way to start the day.

Janey awoke and came into the kitchen, and she ate, too.

When we finished, we helped wash and dry the dishes.

"We'll be gone most of the day," Dad said to me.

"Keep an eye on things. And look after Janey."

"I will," I replied.

Mom and Dad left.

"Alright," I said. "First things first." I explained to John all of the things we had to do. He really sounded eager to get started. I think he liked the idea of having to take care of the animals.

"Janey . . . you stay inside and watch cartoons."

She shook her head.

"Huh-uh," she said. "I want to help, too!"

*Oh, brother,* I thought.

"Fine," I said, placing my hands on my hips. "But if you don't do exactly what I say, I'm going to feed you to the giant duckies."

Her eyes got really big, and then she glared at me. "You're just trying to scare me, you meanie!" she said sharply.

*Drats.* I thought that if I could scare her, she would stay inside and out of our way.

"Let's get started," I said.

We walked outside and into the cool morning. The sun wasn't quite up yet, but the sky was turning shades of yellow and orange and pink. The air was fresh and new.

We walked across the yard and into the driveway. The geese saw us coming and began waddling toward us. They honked and cackled, knowing that they were about to get fed. Other animals were waking up, too. A few cows mooed, and I could hear the hogs rooting around in the pasture on the other side of the barn.

"Janey, you can feed the giant duckies," I said.

"They're *geese!*" she said. "You told me so!".

"I know," I smirked. "I'm just kidding. I'll get you a pail of food, and you can feed them."

John and I walked to the barn, but when I looked inside, I stopped.

So did John.

Something was very, very wrong.

All of the tractors . . . *all of them* . . . were lined up side-by-side, like machine soldiers!

# 13

It was impossible.

Tractors don't move all by themselves.

*"How . . . how did they do that?"* John asked.

I shook my head.

"Dad must have done it," I said.

"No," John answered. "You took the keys!"

John was right.

"Hang on," I said. "Wait here."

I turned and ran back across the driveway, over the yard, and into the house. I raced into my bedroom.

*The keys were still on my dresser!*

I scooped up all of the keys and flew out of the house. John was standing in front of the barn door, staring in amazement at the tractors inside.  Janey was standing by the fence, trying to coax a cow to come closer.  The cow was ignoring her.

I showed John my handful of keys.

"Dad didn't move them, that's for sure," I said.

"What about the workers?" John asked.  "Could one of them have moved the tractors?"

I shook my head.  "No," I said.  "They all have Sunday off.  Besides . . . they would still have to use the keys to get them started."

"Maybe your dad pushed them all by himself."

Again, I shook my head.

"He might have been able to move a couple of the smaller ones," I said.  "But not any of the big ones.  Those things weigh a ton."

Janey gave up on the cow and walked over to us.  By now, the geese had grown impatient.  They were all around us, honking and demanding to be fed.

I scooped up a pail of scratch and gave it to Janey.  'Scratch' is a mix of cracked corn, oats, and wheat.  I know it doesn't sound very good, but the geese go crazy over it.

"Just toss it out onto the ground," I said, and I showed her how to do it by scooping up a handful and scattering the feed.  She took the pail and began her task, giggling with delight.

I turned and looked back at the tractors. There was no explanation as to how they could have moved. It was like they were ready for battle.

All of a sudden, the lights of one of the tractors turned on! They blinked a few times, then went off.

*"Did you—"*

*"Yes,"* John gulped, interrupting me. *"I saw it."*

The lights flashed again!

"What's going on?!?!" John asked incredulously. "How is that tractor doing that?!?!"

"It *can't,"* I whispered. "That's all there is to it. It just . . . *can't."*

The headlights turned on, then off. Then on again.

"Wait a minute," I said. "Maybe there's a problem with the wiring. That might cause it to do that."

I started towards the tractor.

*Yeah, that's it,* I thought. *Bad wiring. I can just disconnect the battery and—*

Without warning, a tractor roared to life, it's motor revving and racing! Then another . . . *and another!*

And when they started to move all by themselves, I knew right then and there that we were in a lot of trouble.

61

# 14

We didn't say a thing. The three of us whirled and ran out of the barn as fast as we could. I didn't even glance over my shoulder.

I just wanted *out of there.*

I wanted out of there, and in the house where we would be safe.

*How can that be?* I thought as I raced across the yard. *How can those things start on their own? And move all by themselves?*

It was like they were . . . *alive.* Like the tractors had somehow come to life after a long sleep.

I was at the door first, and I threw it open, holding it for John and Janey. When they were safely inside the house, I bolted through the door and slammed it closed behind me.

In the barn, we could hear the tractors revving and roaring.

"Look!" John exclaimed, pointing out the window.

The three of us huddled together, watching the strange scene in the driveway.

The tractors were leaving the barn! They were driving out under their own power! They chugged along slowly weaving around the driveway and the yard. One of the tractors was raising and lowering its front bucket. Another was blowing smoke from its exhaust stack and revving its engine.

It was *crazy!* Machines can't do that! Not all by themselves, they can't!

Other things had come to life, too. The push lawnmower from the garage came into view, whirring like crazy, whizzing back and forth across the driveway and the yard.

"What's going on?" John wondered aloud.

"This is scary," Janey said.

"No kidding," I said. "I can't believe we're seeing this!"

The tractors were getting closer and closer to the house. They weren't moving real fast, but there was a  pattern to what they were doing.

They were ganging up on us.

The tractors gathered together in the front yard like a metal mob, as if they were going to wait for us to come out.

Yeah, right! Like I was going anywhere *near* those things!

This was a nightmare. I kept telling myself that it was all a bad dream . . . but I knew it wasn't.

I knew what I was seeing.

Tractors had come to life. Terrible Tractors were threatening to take over the entire ranch . . . and there was nothing we could do about it!

We stood in the living room, staring out the window for a long time.

"How could this happen?" John asked again.

"I don't know," I said, shaking my head. I looked at him. "It's impossible. I mean . . . it's really *impossible.* Machines can't do this. They can't come to life like this!"

"Well, seeing is believing," John said. "And I know what I'm seeing."

And then it hit me.

*"The experimental fuel!"* I cried. *"That has to be it!"*

"The experimental fuel?" John replied.

"Yes! Remember yesterday when we filled up all

65

of the equipment?"

John nodded.

"Well," I continued, "that has to be it! There must be something in the fuel that is making these things come alive!"

"That's crazy!" John said.

"Hey, you just said that seeing is believing," I replied. "And I'm seeing the same thing you are."

"Looky!" cried Janey. She pointed and gasped.

"Oh my gosh!" I cried.

"Holy cow!" John breathed.

And when I saw what Janey was pointing at, I freaked.

*"No!"* I whispered. *"No, no NO!!!!"*

# 15

From behind the barn, a piece of heavy equipment was emerging.

A yellow bulldozer with black letters. Then a big yellow backhoe.

*Oh no! The heavy machinery from behind the barn!*

We were in trouble way over our heads.

All around the ranch, the tractors and farm equipment were creating havoc. They began digging holes and tearing up the driveway. They knocked down part of the corral, and cows were fleeing in panic. The geese were running all over the place, honking wildly.

It was *madness*. Complete and total *madness*.

"Do you really think that the fuel has something to do with this?" John asked.

"I can't think of anything else," I replied.

"It's like they have a mind of their own," Janey said.

And she was right. It was as if the tractors—and the rest of the equipment that I had filled with the experimental fuel—now had their own brains.

Trouble was . . . *what were they up to? What did they want? What were they after?*

*Us?*

The bulldozer was busy plowing dirt, pushing it away from the barn. It had demolished Mom's small flower garden. When Mom saw that, she was going to go bananas!

"Uh oh," John said. "Look."

The bulldozer had stopped its plowing, and it turned toward our house.

Toward *us.*

"I don't like the looks of this at all," I said, eyeing the tractor suspiciously.

Slowly, it began to move in our direction, and my heart started pounding even harder.

"I don't think he likes us," Janey said.

I wasn't sure what was happening, but I sure didn't like the looks of things. All of the other tractors had stopped moving . . . except for the yellow bulldozer.

It was like they were watching the big piece of farm equipment, waiting for it to do something.

And as we watched, the dozer came closer.

It was *huge.*

It was *alive.*

It was huge, it was alive . . . *and it was headed right for our house!*

# 16

This wasn't a nightmare.

It was *worse.*

Not only had the tractors in the barn come alive, but the enormous dozers and cranes had, too!

*And one was heading right for our house!*

"We've got to get out of here!" I said.

"Out of here?!?!" John cried. "Where are we going to go?!?!? Those machines will have us for lunch!"

*Think, Jake, think,* I ordered myself.

I went to the phone and picked it up.

No dial tone. The tractors must have cut the underground phone line.

I ran to the back of the house and looked outside.

"This way!" I shouted.

John and Janey bounded through the house.

"There aren't any tractors behind the house!" I said. "We can make a run for it and head for our neighbor's home! The Millers live on the other side of that ridge!"

John peered out the window. "That looks like it's a long ways away," he said.

"It's about a quarter of a mile," I assured him. "I know the Millers really well. If we can get there, we can call for help. Besides . . . we can't stay here!"

John didn't have to think much longer.

"Okay, let's do it," he said. "Janey . . . hang on to my hand and don't let go."

"Okay," she said. For as young as she was, she wasn't as frightened as I thought she would be.

Which was probably a good thing. The last thing we needed was a freaked-out little girl, screaming and crying her head off.

I opened the back door and stuck my head out.

*"The coast is clear!"* I hissed. *"Let's go!"*

The three of us bolted out the back door.

*Man, I hope I'm right about this,* I thought. *I really, really, REALLY hope I'm right about this.*

Our feet pounded the gravel road. I could hear the tractors on the other side of our house, but as we ran farther and farther away, their sounds faded. I wondered if the bulldozer had smashed into our house yet.

Halfway there. John was right behind me, and Janey was running as fast as her little legs could take her. She was clutching tightly to John's hand, just like he'd told her to.

And then we were in the Miller's driveway. I managed a quick glance behind me, expecting to see a tractor chasing us. I was really relieved when I didn't see one.

*"We're going to make it!"* I shouted. *"We're almost there!"*

We ran up the driveway and to the front door. Again, I shot a nervous glance behind me, just to be sure there wasn't a tractor on our tail.

Nothing.

I pounded on the door with my fist.

*"Mr. Miller!"* I shouted. *"Help! We need help!"* I pounded some more, and rang the doorbell a few times. The doorbell didn't work, so I banged on the door again.

*Just our luck,* I thought. *There's nobody home!*

*"Mr. Miller?!?!? Mrs. Miller?!?! Are you home?!?!?"*

There were no sounds from inside the house.

I grasped the doorknob . . . and it turned! The

door opened!

Now, normally, I wouldn't just open up a door to someone's home and go inside. You probably wouldn't, either.

But this was *different*.

This was an *emergency*. A matter of life and death. And besides . . . it was the Millers. Mr. And Mrs. Miller are like grandparents to me.

"It's open!" I cried joyfully. "We can use the phone!"

The three of us went inside. I've been in the Millers's house a lot, and I knew right where the phone was.

I ran to it and picked it up, and my hope went down the drain.

There was no dial tone!

*Oh no! The Millers's phone was dead, too!* The tractors must have cut all the lines up by our house!

Sure enough, when I flicked a light switch, nothing happened.

"They cut the electrical wires," I said.

"I'm shocked," John said.

*"This isn't a time for jokes!"* I snapped. "Let's get out of here! There's another house farther down the road. It's about a mile away . . . but we have to try and make it."

"I don't think we'll be able to," John said. "Look." He pointed out the window, and I saw the last thing in the world that I wanted to see.

A tractor.

It was green and yellow.

There was no one driving it.

And it was on the dirt road, headed in our direction!

# 17

"They know we're here!" I exclaimed.

"We have to get out of here," John said. His gazed followed the tractor as it ambled toward the house.

I shook my head. "Not with that thing coming!" I said. "There's no way we'd be able to out run it."

The green and yellow tractor turned into the driveway.

"Don't these people have a tractor? Or a car or something?"

A light went on in my head. Bells clanged.

*"John! That's it!"*

His eyes flashed. "What?" he asked. "Do they have a car?"

I shook my head. "No, not a car. A *tractor!* Mr. Miller has a tractor in his shed!"

I glanced at the tractor coming down the driveway, and then turned and looked at the shed. It wasn't far from the house.

"I can make it," I said. "I can make it to the shed before that tractor gets here."

"What do you want us to do?" John asked.

"Nothing," I replied. "Just stay here."

"But . . . but I thought that we would use the tractor to escape," John said.

"Yeah," said Janey. "I wanna go home!" She sniffled and I thought she was going to cry, but she didn't.

"I'll see if I can fend off this tractor using Mr. Miller's tractor," I said. "It's not very fast, I'm afraid. But if I can stop that other tractor somehow, then maybe we can use the Millers's tractor to get away."

I bolted out the front door. The green and yellow tractor was coming down the driveway. Smoke was pouring out of its exhaust stack, and I couldn't help but notice that it looked like it had a *face.*

Not a real face, of course.

But a *machine* face. With eyes and teeth and everything.

In seconds I was at the shed. The big garage-type

door rolled up easily, and I rushed inside.

Bingo! Mr. Millers' tractor was parked right where it belonged!

I jumped up and into the seat.

*Double bingo! The keys were in the ignition!*

Maybe this was my lucky day, after all.

Outside, I could hear the green and yellow tractor getting closer and closer.

I turned the key, and the motor chugged to life. My hand found the gear shift and I slipped it into reverse, turned my head, and guided the tractor out of the shed.

And just in time, too. The green and yellow tractor was nearly at the shed, and if I had waited any longer, it could have blocked me inside.

Now, I had a fighting chance.

And a *plan*.

Tractors run on *fuel*. I had a good notion that the experimental fuel was causing the tractors to act the way they did.

And tractors need *electricity*. They need a *battery*.

If I could somehow get the tractor turned over so its wheels wouldn't touch the ground, then it couldn't move. I could run up to it and disconnect the battery!

I knew it was going to be difficult, but it was the only way I could think to stop the rampaging machine.

*Wham!* The tractor slammed into the side of Mr. Miller's tractor. I spun the wheel and pressed on the gas pedal, and whirled away.

Now it was my turn.

I cranked the wheel as hard as I could, pointing it in the direction of the green and yellow tractor. It hadn't had a chance to turn and come after me, and I pressed the gas pedal as far as it would go.

Mr. Miller's tractor shot forward, slamming into the metal beast.

Clearly, it hadn't been prepared. The jolt knocked the green and yellow tractor sideways, and it almost—*almost*—rolled over!

*My plan might work, after all!*

But now it was the green and yellow tractor's turn.

Without any warning, the tractor backed away and reared up like a horse! Angry smoke spewed from the exhaust stack. The motor snarled like a bear.

*And it charged at me!*

Its front wheels were up in the air, and its motor was racing and revving.

I couldn't react in time. The green and yellow tractor had caught me off guard, and I didn't even have time to throw my machine into reverse.

And then—

It was too late. The tractor was suddenly looming over me like an attacking elephant. Its front wheels slammed into my shoulder, and the impact sent me flying from the tractor. It felt like I had been kicked by a horse.

I hit the ground with a heavy thud. The blow knocked the wind from me, but I wasn't hurt—*yet.*

I was about to be.

I rolled over and looked up . . . just in time to see the giant metal monster above me, reared up in a strike position.

There was a roar from its engine, a thundering nasty snarl—and the tractor attacked.

# 18

It was all over for me, and that's all there was to it. In a single, swift motion, the monster tractor came at me.

I knew that it was pointless, but I snapped sideways and tried to roll away.

But I was sure I wouldn't make it. The tractor was too close, and it was too fast.

I closed my eyes.

*Ker-CRASH!* The front two tractor tires slammed into the earth in an explosion of thundering metal and rubber.

I opened my eyes.

By some miracle, the tires had missed me! I had rolled sideways . . . right between the two tires!

I could feel the heat of the engine above me, and I could smell the thick, oily exhaust.

And I didn't wait another instant.

The tractor had already started to move, but I was able to jump up and get out of its way. Mr. Miller's tractor was only a few yards away and I ran to it, springing up and into the seat. It was still running, and I wheeled it around and floored the gas pedal.

And it was a good thing, too . . . because the green and yellow tractor was charging again. This time I was able to get out of its way.

I spun the steering wheel around, and Mr. Miller's tractor whirled about.

The other tractor hadn't had a chance to turn around for another attack . . . and I wasn't going to give it a chance.

I slammed the gas pedal down as far as it would go, and charged directly at the side of the tractor.

*BAM!*

The impact was loud, and I almost fell from my seat.

But the result was what I was hoping for.

I had succeeded in knocking the tractor off its balance. One of its rear wheels came off the ground, and I hit the gas again, pushing, the tractor more and more.

*There!*

In a terrible symphony of crunching metal, the green and yellow tractor fell sideways on the ground. Its wheels spun like mad, but it was powerless to go anywhere.

Nevertheless, it looked like it was trying to right itself. The tractor tried to scramble sideways, tried to get one of its tires to dig into the ground enough so that it could spin itself up. It reminded me of a giant steel turtle on its back, legs flailing, trying to turn itself over.

There was a noise from inside the house, and I turned my head.

John and Janey were cheering, and I raised my fist in the air in victory.

But I knew it wasn't over yet.

And I knew what I would have to do. It might be dangerous, but I had to do it.

I left Mr. Miller's tractor running and climbed down.

The green and yellow tractor was still upside down, running, its tires spinning aimlessly.

*Disconnect the battery,* I thought. *Then, open up the gas tank and let all of the fuel drain out. It worked before. It'll work again.*

It was a daring plan, but I thought it just might do

the trick.

Step by cautious step, I walked toward the struggling tractor.

# 19

I must have looked pretty silly, the way I approached the upended tractor. I walked toward it like I was walking toward a vicious animal.

And, in a way, that's what it was.

An *animal.* A bloodthirsty, metal animal.

I could see the battery cables protruding from the side of the engine housing. I wouldn't have the time to try and open up the casing, so I decided to simply grab the cables and yank them from the battery.

The green and yellow tractor was still struggling to right itself.

I took a breath and lunged for it, arms outstretched, reaching for the cable wires . . .

*Got them!*

I yanked as hard as I could.

There was a sudden *snap* as the wires broke away from the battery terminal.

The result was immediate. The tractor's motor stopped almost instantly, and fell silent. The big rear wheels continued to spin, but they were slowing quickly.

*It worked!*

I breathed a huge sigh of relief.

*"You did it!"* John shouted. He and Janey were already out the door and racing across the gravel driveway.

The Texas sun was hot, and I was really sweating now. Perspiration glossed my skin and dampened my shirt. I wiped my brow and looked at the lifeless tractor.

"One down," John said, as he reached my side.

"Not quite," I replied. "I want to make sure that this one is finished for good. Stay back, just in case."

John and Janey stood a few feet away as I walked around the hulking machine. I was still a bit leery, wondering if the tractor would suddenly come to life and spring up.

*Maybe it's trying to trick us,* I pondered. *Maybe it only* wanted *me to think it was dead.* I was going to have to be careful.

The gas cap was on the side of the tractor, and I turned it and opened up the tank.

Immediately, fuel began to spill out. I drew my hand away quickly, so as not to get any of the oily green liquid on myself.

The fuel sprayed out onto the ground, covering the dirt and clumps of grass.

The three of us gasped. I had thought that the fuel would just seep into the ground.

But that's not what happened.

That's not what happened at all . . . .

# 20

*The fuel burned the ground!*

That's right. It *burned* the ground! It was one of the freakiest things I had ever seen in my life.

It was like acid had been poured on the ground. There was a hissing sound like frying bacon. Smoke rose up from the dirt, and pea-green bubbles boiled and simmered in the gravel.

And suddenly—

*Screaming.*

It began as a low shriek, a whining sound, but it grew louder and louder and louder. The more the fuel tank emptied onto the ground, the louder the shrieking grew. It was as if the tractor was howling a final, dying gasp.

Janey looked like she had seen a ghost. Her mouth was open, and she placed her hands over her ears.

John was equally shocked, and he, too, placed his hands over his ears.

I took a few steps back, just to be safe. I had no idea what might happen next.

The three of us watched as the tractor continued its unearthly wailing. Liquid continued spilling onto the ground, causing a cloud of misty green smoke to rise up into the sky.

Finally, the fuel tank was empty. The screeching stopped, and the fizzing fuel on the ground stopped bubbling and popping.

The three of us were silent for a moment. A bug flew by my ear and I swished it away.

John walked to my side, inspecting the ground and the lifeless tractor. He shook his head slowly.

"Dude, your dad is gonna freak when he sees this," he said.

John was right, that was for sure. Dad was going to blow his top when he saw what the tractors had done to the farm.

But I wasn't worried about that now. Now, the only thing I could think about was the three of us climbing onto Mr. Miller's tractor and going to get help.

But it wasn't going to be that simple.

There was a sudden roar, and it startled me. The three of us spun and looked down the road.

Another tractor was coming . . . and *fast!*

# 21

Janey screamed, and ran back to the house.

*"Janey!"* I shouted out to her. *"No! No!"*

But it was too late. Janey had already reached the house, and had gone inside.

*"Quick!"* I ordered John. *"Get onto the tractor!"*

John and I scrambled up the tractor. The seat wasn't big enough for both of us, so I sat and steered while John held onto the side of the tractor, his feet planted on a metal ladder rung. I hit the gas, and the motor roared.

"What are we going to do?!?!" John shouted above the thundering engine.

"Well, we can't leave Janey alone," I said, "so we can't go and get help. Let's try and take out this tractor!"

I recognized the all-yellow tractor with a large bail in the front. This was the one Dad usually uses to dig ditches or big holes.

Not today! That thing was coming after us, and quick.

"Here's what we'll do," I said loudly. "See that embankment over there?"

John followed my gaze.

"Yeah," he said.

"There's a pond just on the other side. We'll head for it. If the yellow tractor chases us, maybe we can swerve just before we reach the pond."

"And the yellow tractor won't be able to stop!" John exclaimed.

"That's what I'm hoping for," I said.

And I wasn't going to have any problems getting the yellow tractor to chase us! He was coming down the driveway, full throttle, right at us!

"Hang on!" I shouted to John, and I punched the gas pedal to the floor. Huge tires spit gravel as we flew forward, over a pasture and past the shed. The ride was bumpy, and it was all I could do to hang on to the steering wheel.

John shot a glance behind us. *It's gaining on us!* he screamed.

*"I'm going as fast as I can!"* I replied. *"This thing won't go any faster!"*

I focused on the embankment. If we could make it there with the yellow tractor right behind us, I could turn sharply at the last minute . . . and the pursuing tractor, I hoped, would go splashing into the pond.

Suddenly, there was a loud *crash!* and our tractor lurched forward.

*"FASTER!"* John screamed. *"It's hitting us! The thing is attacking!"*

We were almost to the pond. Only another few feet.

*Crash!* The tractor slammed into us again, and this time the jolt almost knocked John off. I had to grab his arm to keep him from flying from the tractor!

We reached the embankment. Before us was a short, steep hill that led right to a muddy pond.

*Now or never,* I thought.

I spun the steering wheel with everything I had. The sudden turn caused our tractor to lurch sideways. John screamed, and he almost flew off again.

I straightened out the wheel and let my foot off the gas.

*"It worked!"* John suddenly cried. *"Look!"*

Behind us, the yellow tractor had tried to turn at

the last moment, but it was too late. It teetered sideways, wobbled . . . and fell! It didn't go into the pond like I thought it would, but we had stopped it from chasing us!

And it wasn't going anywhere, either. It was on its side and its wheels were spinning like mad pinwheels. The engine was furious, and it snarled and growled as it tried to right itself.

*"The battery cable!"* I shouted.

I wheeled the tractor around and pulled to a stop near the embankment. John and I leapt off and raced to the yellow tractor.

To get at the battery cable I had to go on the other side of the tractor, which meant that I had to go into the pond. I didn't even take my shoes off. I trudged through knee-deep water until I reached the engine case, which was partially in the water. The battery cables were in plain view, and in one single motion I grabbed them and yanked.

The engine died immediately, and John and I heaved a sigh of relief.

I reached over and unscrewed the gas cap, once again being careful not to get any of the dangerous liquid on myself. When I pulled off the cap, I trudged quickly out of the pond and back to the shore.

Green, acid-like fuel spilled into the water, again

creating a smelly cloud. There was a terrible shrieking sound, just like the green and yellow tractor. It was eerie.

The green fuel looked like soup in the water. It foamed and hissed and bubbled and popped.

"If that's not pollution, I don't know what is," John said.

And he was right. The spilled fuel wasn't going to be very good for the pond, that was for sure.

But, at the time, we had no choice. We were battling mean metal monsters, and it was a fight to the finish. It was us or them.

"Let's get out of here before another one comes," I said. "We'll get your sister, and then we'll go."

We climbed back onto the tractor and headed back to the house, on the lookout for more tractors. We didn't see any, and my hope grew.

*We're going to make it,* I told myself. *We're going to make it now. We'll pick up Janey and go get help.*

I drove the tractor right up to the front door.

"Janey!" John shouted from the tractor. "Come on! We're leaving!"

Janey didn't come to the door.

"Janey!" John shouted again.

Still no Janey.

"Go get her!" I ordered. "Before another tractor

comes after us!"

John was scrambling off the tractor when I shot a nervous glance over my shoulder. I expected to see a tractor, coming down the road at full speed.

What I didn't expect was what I actually *did* see.

*Janey.*

She was running up the gravel road . . . *heading back to my house!*

# 22

"*JANEY!*" I screamed. But I knew she was too far away to hear me.

"What is she doing?!?!?" John stammered.

"*I don't know, but we have to stop her!*" I shouted. "*Come on!*"

John scrambled onto the tractor. I backed up the machine, spun it around, and set out.

Janey was near the top of the hill as we tore out of the driveway. Man . . . if there was ever a time that we needed this tractor to go fast, it was now!

Janey disappeared over the crest of the hill, but we were gaining fast. Maybe we would reach her before she got much farther.

*Why?!?!* I wondered. *Why is she running back to*

*our house? Back to all of those creepy tractors?*

We reached the hill, and Janey came into view. She was still running, her legs churning across the gravel, heading toward our house.

We were going to make it. We would reach her in a few seconds, pick her up, and turn around.

*Maybe she thinks that she's running for help,* I thought. That made the most sense. Maybe she thought that she was running to safety.

And then I saw something that made my skin crawl. My blood ran cold, and I felt like the air in my lungs had been yanked out.

John's arm shot out, pointing.

*"Oh no!!!!!"* he shouted. *"Janey!! Janey!! Look out!"*

It was a tractor, and I recognized it right away. It was Dad's favorite: a 1954 John Deere. It was big and green with bright yellow rims. The rear tires were twice my height, and the front two tires were about the size of car tires, but they were set close together. Dad had bought the tractor a few years ago and rebuilt it himself. It was his special tractor, and sometimes he drove it just for fun, like someone would ride a bike or a motorcycle.

Only now, no one was driving it. The huge John Deere had come alive, and it had a mind of its own.

Black smoke poured from the exhaust stack mounted at the front of the tractor.

And it looked *angry*.

It looked *mean* and it looked *nasty*.

But even worse . . . it seemed to be looking at Janey . . . and it was heading directly toward her!

# 23

We were moving as fast as we could. The big green John Deere was running at full speed, but it wasn't as fast as Mr. Miller's tractor.

But the John Deere was closer to John's sister than we were.

*"Janey!!!"* John screamed over the roar of the churning motor.

Whether or not she heard him, I don't know. But right after he shouted to her, Janey noticed the enormous green tractor bearing down on her. She suddenly began running the other way, back toward us.

*Thank goodness,* I thought. *At least she's running in the opposite direction.*

I could see our house now. There were still tractors driving all around. The big dozers and backhoes were steaming all around the ranch, digging holes and creating small mountains. They'd even torn a huge hole in the side of the barn. So far, however, it didn't look like they'd damaged our home.

We were getting close to Janey. The big green John Deere was behind her, but now we were closer to Janey than it was.

We were going to make it.

I slowed the tractor. Janey ran up to the side and John reached down. He clasped her outstretched hand and yanked her off the ground in a single, swift motion.

She was safe!

*"Go!"* John shouted as the green John Deere continued to bear down on us. I spun the tractor around to make our escape.

But we weren't going *anywhere*.

Not *yet,* anyway.

Somehow, one of the tractors had come up behind us. It had probably been waiting and planning, and now it was heading up the gravel road, coming our way!

I looked across the field. It was bumpy and torn

up, and if we tried to outrun the other tractors by cutting across it, we'd never make it.

I looked on the other side of the road. Here, the land was undeveloped. There were trees and a few rocks that dotted the sparse, tiny forest. Maybe we could weave through the tree trunks and escape the charging tractors.

"Hang on!" I shouted. "This is going to be bumpy!"

I wheeled Mr. Miller's tractor off the gravel road, through a steep ditch, and through a patch of brush. Then I turned and circled around a big tree, and then another.

"What were you thinking back there?!?!" John finally asked Janey. "Why were you running back to Jake's house?!?!?"

"I remembered that the geese were hungry," Janey answered. "I was worried about them."

*Good grief.* I mean, it was a nice thought and all. But for gosh sakes . . . she had placed herself in a lot of danger. The geese were going to have to wait to be fed.

I wound the tractor around trees like a slithering snake. Behind us, the other two machines were following, but they were bumping into trees and it was slowing them down.

There was a large tree in front of us, and I turned the wheel to maneuver around it.

*Bam!* I hit the tree. The impact almost knocked all three of us from the machine.

I threw the tractor into reverse and backed away from the tree. I turned and tried to go the other direction.

*The space wasn't big enough!*

I would have to back up, turn around, and find another place in the woods to cut through. I thought that we could still outrun the other two tractors, but not if we got stuck in another corner like we had.

I turned the big machine, and we began heading in another direction . . . but once again, I found us caught in the thick trees.

And suddenly, I realized that my plan wasn't going to work. I had thought that it would be the other two tractors that would get stuck, but that wasn't the case. The trees were too thick even for *me* to maneuver through.

We would have to go back out to the road and try to outrun the two tractors.

I turned once again, and wove Mr. Miller's tractor on a course for the gravel road. The other two tractors changed their courses as well, and headed out of the trees.

Next to me, John and Janey held onto the tractor with all of their strength. John grasped the tractor with one hand. With the other, he held onto Janey's arm—just in case she lost her own grip on the machine.

We bounced through the ditch and onto the gravel road. Right behind us, the big green John Deere was in pursuit.

And in front of us, the other tractor suddenly bounded up from the ditch.

Both tractors were coming at us! Smoke poured from their exhaust pipes, and their motors roared like furious jet engines.

Janey screamed in horror. John gasped. The tractors were speeding toward us.

*Oh no! We were going to be sandwiched in between them! We were going to be crushed like bugs!*

# 24

I did the only thing I could do. I knew that avoiding the two tractors was probably impossible, but I hoped that I could at least turn the tractor in such a way that the two attacking machines wouldn't hit us.

I slammed the gas pedal to the floor and cranked the wheel around. Our tractor shot forward and sideways, and, once again, John had to grab Janey to keep her from flying off.

And then—

A lucky break.

*The two tractors missed us! We had been able to squeeze out of their way, just in the nick of time!*

But what happened next was even better. The two tractors, traveling fast and unable to stop, slammed into one another!

There was a thunderous explosion of grinding metal. Sparks flew like fireworks.

One of the tractors spun sideways and fell over. One of its wheels had completely broken off, and it careened down the ditch, bounced off of a tree, and rolled to a stop.

The other tractor, the big green and yellow John Deere, appeared to be dazed. It rolled backwards slowly, like it was injured . . . which, of course, it was.

I seized the opportunity to strike.

*"Hang on tight!"* I shouted to John and Janey. I cranked the wheel again, steered right at the tractor, and hit the gas.

Our tractor shot forward. There was another explosion of metal as we slammed into the side of the big John Deere. This time, the collision was so great that neither John nor Janey could hold on. They lost their grip and tumbled to the hard ground.

But my plan had worked. The John Deere, unable to get out of the way, was sent careening sideways. The big machine staggered on two wheels for a moment before crashing on its side.

Wheels spun and dirt flew. Dust whirled like a tornado.

Now we had a fighting chance, and John knew it, too. He was already racing to the first tractor that had been knocked over. I stopped the machine I was driving, climbed down, and raced to the hobbled John Deere. I grabbed the battery cables and yanked, found the gas cap and gave it a twist. Green fuel gushed out.

Once again, the machines seemed to scream and protest as the strange liquid spilled to the ground. It boiled and burned, and pea-green steam rose from the dirt.

*"Look!"* Janey suddenly cried above the shrieking tractors. She was pointing up the road, toward our house.

And I did *not* like what I saw.

# 25

It wasn't a tractor.

It was a front end loader.

An *enormous* front end loader. This was one of the giant machines that were behind the barn. It was all yellow and had four gigantic tires. It had a big bucket in the front for picking up dirt and other heavy objects. The bucket looked like an over-sized bathtub. The entire piece of equipment was nearly as tall as our house, and three times the size of a car.

And it was coming toward us . . . *fast.*

"Let's get out of here!" I shouted. "Get on the tractor! Quick!"

I raced to Mr. Miller's tractor, and John did, too. He and I made it to the machine at the same time.

Janey was right behind John, and none of us wasted any time climbing onto the tractor.

"Are we going to be able to outrun that thing?!?!" John shouted.

I stepped on the gas and whirled the tractor around, heading us away from the oncoming front end loader.

"Yes!" I shouted back.

But that wasn't the truth. The truth was, there was *no way* we would be able to outrun the front end loader. Not in Mr. Miller's tractor, anyway.

But I didn't want Janey or John to freak out. I had to think of something . . . and quick.

The gas pedal was floored. We were moving as fast as we could. A nine-banded armadillo was near the shoulder, and he scurried off. We see a lot of armadillos in Texas.

We passed the Miller's home and kept right on going, up the gravel road . . . and that was going to be about as far as we would make it.

"It's almost here!" John shouted. Janey screamed.

I shot a quick glance over my shoulder. The huge front end loader was so close I could almost feel its hot, thick exhaust. Its bucket was raised high, and I couldn't bear to think of that thing coming down on

116

us.

I had to do something. If I waited one more second, the loader would be upon us.

I spun the wheel, and we turned so quick that I thought we were going to roll over. We lurched sideways so violently that one of our rear wheels came off the ground!

But the trick worked. The giant yellow loader flew harmlessly past, unable to maneuver nearly as quickly as we could.

The sudden turn took us off the road. We bounced across the ditch and into the field. I didn't know where we were going; all I knew was that we had to stay away from that awful front end loader.

The field was a maze of holes and bumps. It had been torn up earlier in the year, in preparation for use next spring. There were rocks and bumps and stumps that I had to avoid, and more than once I flew out of my seat and had to hang on to the steering wheel so I didn't get tossed off the tractor.

*"It's coming after us!"* Janey screamed. I snapped my head around, already knowing exactly what I would see.

The gargantuan front end loader was following us across the field . . . and it was gaining with every passing second.

We were traveling as fast as we safely could. There were so many potholes and bumps that it would be impossible to try and increase our speed without risking flipping our tractor over.

Up ahead, I spotted a wide drainage ditch. I hoped that we could speed right through it, because if we had to slow down now, the loader would crush us for sure.

We bounced across the field like crazy. Right behind us, the giant front end loader followed, getting closer and closer and closer.

*"This is going to be bumpy!"* I shouted, warning John and Janey. *"Whatever you do . . . don't let go!"*

Our tractor dove into the ditch. We were going so fast that the front wheels came off the ground . . . but man, when they hit, I thought the entire piece of machinery was going to collapse! I bounced up out of the seat, then slammed back down. It felt like I had been spanked by two thousand pounds of steel.

But we were still moving. I knew that the loader would have to slow down to cross the ditch, and I hit the gas and began to climb up the other side of the incline.

*"STOP!!!"* John shouted. *"STOP! STOP! STOP!"*

I didn't stop. Instead, I turned my head to see what was wrong.

118

I didn't have to ask.

When I turned, I could clearly see that Janey was gone! She had fallen from the tractor when we had crashed into the ditch!

But what I saw behind me was even more horrifying.

Not only had Janey fallen . . . *but she'd been scooped up by the front end loader!*

# 26

This was madness. Complete and total madness. The huge front end loader had scooped Janey up and raised her high into the air!

The enormous machine backed up, spun around, and began heading back to our house.

*"JANEY!"* John screamed. *"HANG ON! WE'LL SAVE YOU!!"*

Neither of us knew how or what we would do. But one thing was for sure: we had to do *something.* Janey was in a lot of danger.

"Chase after it!" John shouted.

I wheeled Mr. Miller's tractor around and gave chase. The hulking yellow machine wasn't going fast, but we still had a hard time catching up to it.

*"Faster!"* John ordered.

*"I'm going as fast as this thing will go!"* I replied.

Soon, we were directly behind the menacing yellow metal beast. Smelly exhaust fumes blew right into my face, and it almost made me sick. I could taste the gritty dry dust in my mouth that the big loader was kicking up. It was getting into my eyes and making them water.

We couldn't see Janey, but we knew she was still in the giant front bucket. Somehow, we had to get her out of there before the mammoth machine got back to our ranch. I wasn't sure what would happen if we failed, but I knew that it wouldn't be good.

*"There's no way I can ram that thing!"* I shouted to John over the roaring engines. *"It's too big!"*

*"Try and get alongside of it!"* John said. *"Try and pull up toward the front of it!"*

I pulled around the side of the huge, rolling beast. At least I didn't have to breathe in the fumes or the dust.

But I wasn't sure if I would be able to make it around to the side. The giant loader nearly took up the entire road!

Somehow, I managed. I was so close to the yellow loader that I could almost reach out and touch it!

And we could see Janey! She was still in the front loader, looking down at us in fright. She looked like she had been crying.

"Hang on Janey!" John screamed. *"I'm going to get you!"*

*Huh?* I thought. *What was he talking about? Janey was ten feet off the ground, and we were going thirty miles an hour!*

"Jake!" John screamed. *"Pull up to the front! Get us under the bucket!"*

"You're crazy!" I shouted back. *"No way! If that bucket comes down, we'll be crushed!"*

"That's my sister up there!" John screamed defiantly. *"That's my sister, and no metal monster is going to swipe her away!"*

There was a fire in his eyes that I'd never seen before. John wasn't just *worried* about Janey . . . he was *infuriated*. At that moment, he could probably arm-wrestle the huge yellow monster—and *win*.

I pulled our tractor up toward the front end of the loader. We were still traveling pretty fast, and we were lurching and jolting all over the place. If I wasn't extra careful, we would smash into the front wheel of the loader.

Then, of course, it would be all over. Mr. Miller's tractor—as well as me and John—would be crushed by twenty tons of tractor.

*"Closer!"* John ordered.

I pulled up alongside and beneath the huge metal bucket. Janey was above us, but there was nothing she could do.

Suddenly, John climbed past me! He climbed onto the engine hood in front of me—and stood up!

*"Janey!"* he shouted. *"Climb over the side and lower yourself down!"*

He was crazy! There was no way his plan would work. He was already having a hard time trying to keep his balance, and when we hit a bump, he slipped and nearly fell.

Janey, however, did as John had ordered. She climbed over the side of the metal bucket, hanging onto the rim with her hands. Her skinny little legs dangled in the air.

John reached up. *"Let go!"* he screamed.

*"I'm scared!"* Janey replied.

The roaring of the engines was deafening.

*"JANEY! LET GO RIGHT NOW! I'll CATCH YOU!"*

Now I was *sure* that John had gone completely out of his mind. This looked like one of the stunts you would see in the movies or on TV.

But on the movies or TV, it wasn't *real*. There were specially trained people who performed the stunts.

What John was doing was *real*.

It was *real* . . . and it was *dangerous*. One slip and he and Janey would both be gone.

*"JANEY!"* he screamed again, only louder this time. *"IF YOU DON'T LET GO RIGHT NOW, IT'S GOING TO BE ALL OVER FOR ALL OF US! I'M TELLING YOU . . . LET . . . GO!"*

And with that, Janey let go of the bucket.

# 27

For an instant, time seemed to stop. For a single moment, I felt like I was watching a slow-motion replay on television.

Janey released her grasp on the bucket . . . and fell right on top of John!

But he was ready for her. His hands were reaching up, and she fell right into his waiting arms.

Now remember: all of this was going on while John was standing on the front of a moving tractor. We were still barreling down the gravel road right next to the front end loader. If, for whatever reason, the front end loader turned our way or lowered its bucket, it would be all over.

John wrapped his arms tightly around his sister

when she dropped down to him. He lost his balance and fell onto the hood of the tractor . . . but neither he nor Janey fell from the machine.

Janey crawled toward me. With one hand, I steered the tractor, and with the other, I reached forward to Janey. She crawled on her hands and knees across the top of the tractor until she reached me. John was right behind her, and he, too, crawled to safety on his hands and knees.

But we weren't out of danger. Not yet, anyway.

Next to us, the giant yellow beast roared along. I knew we had to get away from it, and *fast*.

"Hang tight!" I hollered to John and Janey. They were holding onto the sides of the tractor, their feet planted on the step side.

The first thing I did was hit the brakes. This slowed our tractor quickly, and the front end loader flew on by.

And my spirits were raised. We had been able to rescue Janey without getting crushed by the huge machine.

I whirled the tractor around. Behind us, the big yellow loader continued to amble away. I thought for a moment that it was going to turn around and chase after us, but it didn't. It just kept going . . . which was fine with me!

I glanced over my shoulder. We were very close to our house. In the pasture, tractors and other machines had gathered. It looked like they were holding a meeting or something. The big yellow front end loader had joined with them. Some of the dozers were busy pushing dirt, and a lawnmower was buzzing around in circles.

*"Now we can get out of here!"* I shouted. *"You guys okay?"*

*"Yeah!"* John shouted.

Janey didn't say anything. She just nodded her head. She had been very, very lucky. Despite her dangerous ordeal, she had nothing more than a couple of small scrapes.

I knew that, now, we were going to be okay. I knew we would be able to get away. We would go and get help, and we would be safe.

I pressed the gas pedal down as far as it would go, and the tractor gained in speed . . . for a moment.

Then the engine coughed and sputtered.

The tractor slowed, then sped up again. Then slowed.

"What's going on?" John asked loudly.

I was about to speak when the engine suddenly quit. The tractor rolled to a stop.

"Oh, man!" I shouted, pounding on the steering

wheel. "We're out of gas!"

I turned the key in the ignition. The engine turned over and over, but it wouldn't start.

*"Come on, come on,"* I urged.

But it was useless. The tractor wasn't going anywhere.

Suddenly, we could hear the roar of motors behind us, and we turned our heads to see what was going on.

*Holy cow! Not one . . . but ALL of the tractors and farm equipment were coming our way!*

# 28

Things had just gone from bad—to *worse.*

There must have been over a dozen machines coming toward us! They weren't moving very fast, but just the sight of those creepy contraptions coming our way sent shivers through my whole body.

I looked behind us. The Miller's house was on the other side of the hill, but from where we were, I couldn't even see it. Our house was a lot closer.

And that's where we'd have to go. If we hurried, we had a chance to get to our house and get inside before the menacing machines got to us.

*"To our house!"* I shouted. *"Run around to the back!"*

John grabbed Janey's hand, and the three of us

started out.

"Don't look over your shoulder!" I shouted. "Just keep running! We can make it to the back door of our house!"

The roaring of engines grew louder, and I knew the tractors were getting closer and closer.

However, they weren't going to catch us.

Not this time.

I was the first to reach the back door of our house. I grabbed the knob and flung the door open, then stood aside. Janey and John plunged through, and I immediately followed, slamming the door closed behind me.

"To the basement!" I shouted, hurrying past John and Janey. They followed me as I rushed down the hall and opened up a door.

"Down here!" I pointed to a staircase that led down. I let Janey and John go first, then I closed the door and ran down the steps.

We have a pretty big basement. It's filled with lots of stuff, and Mom keeps telling Dad that he has to start getting rid of it, that we have too much.

"What are we going to do down *here?*" John asked.

I shook my head. "I don't think there's a lot we *can* do," I replied.

"But what if the tractors start attacking the house?" Janey asked.

Again, I shook my head. "I think we're probably safer here than anywhere," I said. "I just hope Mom and Dad get home pretty quick."

Above us, we could hear the roaring of engines all around. The tractors were swarming about like bees around a hive, and I knew that at any moment I'd hear the shattering of glass and the crunching of wood as the vicious vehicles assaulted our house.

Janey sat down on the floor. John sat down on an old folding chair. Junk was piled high all over the place. Old tables, saws, a few fishing poles, toolboxes. On a rickety shelf sat several power tools, a bunch of cans of spray paint, and . . . .

My heart skipped a beat, and I froze for a moment when I saw the item.

*That's it!* I thought. *That's just what we need!*

Our bad luck was finally about to change.

# 29

On the shelf, next to a can of floor wax, was an old CB radio. Dad used to use it all the time, but he hasn't in a while. He even let me play around with it sometimes. I could talk to the truckers that were traveling on the freeway a few miles off.

I had to move some chairs and boxes to reach the shelf.

"What is it?" John asked. He was still sitting in the folding chair.

"It's a CB radio!" I said. "It's battery operated! We might be able to use it to radio for help!"

Hearing the news, John stood up and rushed to where I was.

I picked up the old radio. It was covered with

dust, and I wiped it off with my hand.

"Do you think it still works?" John asked.

"Well, I'm sure the batteries are going to be dead," I replied. I turned the unit over in my hands and popped off the battery cover.

No batteries.

"Oh no!" John cried.

I shook my head. "Actually, that's a good thing," I said. "When batteries get old, some of them leak. They would have ruined the radio. I think I have some batteries upstairs. Stay here."

I handed John the radio, turned, and bounded up the steps. I have a remote control truck that used the same kind of batteries that the radio used, and I had put new batteries in the truck just a few days ago.

I hurried to my bedroom and threw open the closet door.

Hurray!

I felt like shouting. The truck and the remote unit were on the floor in my closet, right where I'd left them!

I picked up the truck, turned it over, and removed the four batteries from the pack. I spun, raced out of my room, and back down the hall.

Outside, the tractors continued their bizarre behavior. They were circling the house, tearing up the yard and the driveway. In the distance, I could see our livestock wandering about in the field. The animals seemed completely uninterested in the goings-on at the farm. It was like it was just another day for them.

I raced back downstairs and retrieved the radio from John.

"Got 'em," I said, showing him the batteries. I popped them into the case, closed the lid, and set the radio down on a table. Janey had stood up, and she walked over to watch.

I pressed the 'on' button.

Lights blinked. A speaker crackled.

*"Yes!"* I shouted. *"It works!"*

"Try it out!" John said.

I picked up the microphone and pressed the key.

*"Mayday! Mayday!"* I said. *"This is Jake Sherwood. All of the tractors on our ranch have come to life! We need help! Mayday!"*

I released the button, and the three of us listened anxiously for a response.

Seconds ticked by. There was a bit of static and some crackling, but then there was nothing.

Suddenly, the speaker came to life. It splattered and sputtered, and a voice came through!

"Uh, Roger that, Jake," a deep, male voice

boomed. "You'd better quit playing around and get off the air!"

*Playing around?!?!?* I thought. *I'm not playing around! I was dead serious!*

I keyed the microphone again.

"This is Jake! I'm not kidding around! We need help!" Again, I explained that the farm equipment had come to life, and I gave him the address to our house. I let off the mic key and waited for a reply.

"Listen, you little kid," the voice angrily shot back. "The radio isn't for goofing around! Someone might have an emergency, and you're creating a disturbance!"

*Little kid?!?!?* I thought. *Who is he calling a little kid?!?!?*

I keyed the microphone and spoke.

"We *do* have an emergency!" I shouted into the mic. "And the disturbance is right here! I'm telling you . . . we need *help! We need—*"

I was interrupted by an awful crash outside! The noise was so loud it shook the house. It sounded like something had exploded!

"Stay here!" I ordered Janey and John. "I'll go see!"

I ran up the steps, bounded into the living room, looked out the window . . . and gasped.

What I saw was horrible.  No . . . it was *worse*.
*Worse* than horrible.

I realized that now the tractors had only been playing with us.

Now, the games were over.

The games were over . . . and the *real* trouble was about to begin.

# 30

*The tractors had demolished the entire barn!*

The entire structure had come down in a heaping pile. Boards and pieces of machinery were all over the place. Dozers were pushing around the fallen timbers!

I ran back downstairs . . . and it happened.

There was another earth-shattering crash, and the entire house shook.

*The tractors were attacking the house!*

The crash was so abrupt, so sudden that John jumped . . . and dropped the radio. It bounced off the edge of the table and smashed to the ground, splintering into a dozen pieces.

"Oh no!" John exclaimed. "Oh no! Now I've

really done it!"

I guess I was mad at John for dropping the radio, but, then again, it wasn't *his* fault. It was an accident. I might have done the same thing.

Janey had tears in her eyes. She was really frightened, and I couldn't blame her. I was awfully scared myself!

"We've got to do something," I said. "We can't stay here in the basement. The whole house is going to fall in on us!"

"I wish that darned tractor hadn't run out of gas," John said dejectedly. "We'd be a long ways away by now."

A thought suddenly hit me like a truck.

*"Gas!"* I shouted. I slapped my palm to my forehead. *"There's a five-gallon can of gas in the garage that's almost full!"*

"But . . . how are we going to fill the tractor?" John asked.

There was a crash as yet another tractor slammed into the house.

"We create a diversion," I replied. "You go out and do something to get the attention of the tractors. When you do, I'll slip around the other side of the house with the can of gas."

"I'm not going out there with those things," John

replied, shaking his head.

"John, it's our last chance," I pleaded. "If I can get the gas to Mr. Miller's tractor, we still could use it to get away."

Janey hadn't said anything in some time, and now she spoke up.

"Don't be such a chicken," was all she said.

John glared at her. "I am not being a chicken," he said defiantly. "And besides, I'm *older* than you. Don't talk to me like that."

"Okay," Janey said. "I apologize. I'm sorry you're a chicken."

John's face grew red. He was about to say something to his sister when I intervened.

"John," I said, "we don't have time for this. We need to act fast. Will you do it?"

John looked into my eyes, then he looked over at Janey. Then he looked back at me.

"Okay," he said. "But I hope it works."

"Remember when you told me to drive up alongside that huge yellow machine?" I asked.

He nodded. "Yeah?"

"I thought you were crazy. I never thought you would be able to do what you did. But I trusted you. And you saved your sister."

He looked at Janey again, and then at me.

Suddenly, there was another earth-shattering crunch from upstairs. The house was being torn to shreds.

"Let's do it," John said bravely. "Let's get gas in that tractor and get out of here."

And the plan was made. John would go out the back door where there weren't any tractors. He would creep around the side of the house. Hopefully, when they saw him, they would chase after him, leaving the front of the house. He would need to run to the backdoor and get back inside before one of the crazy machines got him.

And, of course, while the tractors were chasing John, I would carry the gas can to Mr. Miller's tractor that still sat on the road. John would wait inside, and when he saw me throw the gas can, then he would know to grab Janey and run to the tractor. I would start it up, and we would high-tail it out of there.

Crazy plan? You bet.

But at least it was a plan. And right now, it was our last hope no matter how crazy it seemed.

John and I both went out the back door. Janey waited by the porch, inside.

"You go that way," I pointed, "and I'll go this way. We can do this John. I know we can."

"I know we can," he said hopefully.

144

He turned and walked one way, and I walked the other.  We could hear the roaring of the tractors in front of the house, tearing at pieces of the wrecked barn.  Thankfully, they hadn't destroyed any more of the house.

I took one last look at John.  He gave me a thumbs up, and disappeared around the corner.

Ready or not, the plan was in motion . . . and there was no turning back.

# 31

As I crept around the side of the house, I knew immediately that our plan was working. I watched as two of the tractors and a bulldozer suddenly stopped, turned, and charged off toward the other side of the house. Even the other tractors had taken notice.

*Okay,* I thought. *They've seen John. They've seen him, and now they're going after him.*

I set out across the lawn, hoping that none of the tractors and machinery in the field would take notice. They seemed busy plowing up the dirt. Some of the tractors were just driving around in circles.

Running with the heavy gas can was hard. It was really bulky, and I had to use both hands to carry the thing.

But I hardly noticed it. My eyes never left Mr. Miller's stalled tractor on the road. Soon, I was standing next to the big motor, pouring gas into the tank.

I shot an anxious glance behind me. So far, so good. No tractors were coming my direction. I hoped that John and Janey were doing okay. I sure could hear a lot of roaring and noise coming from behind the house.

The can emptied, and I threw it to the ground. The first part of the plan was a success; I had been able to get to Mr. Miller's tractor and refill the gas tank.

Now, the tricky part. John and Janey would have to make it safely to me before we could escape.

I leapt up onto the tractor, grabbed the keys, and turned them. The engine churned and churned.

*Not today*, I thought. *Please not today. Start. Come on . . . start!*

Suddenly, I heard a loud roar coming from behind the house.

*"Why won't you start?!?!"* I screamed at the tractor. *"Why now?!?!?"*

The engine coughed and hiccoughed, but it didn't start.

*"Please start,"* I begged. *"Oh, please, please*

*start."*

The noise from the house was suddenly very loud. I snapped my head around.

*It was a bulldozer! He was coming right at me!*

# 32

I was just about ready to bail out when Mr. Miller's tractor suddenly caught. The motor thundered to life, and I couldn't believe my luck.

But that didn't solve all of the problems. The big yellow dozer was coming right for me, and there was still no sign of John or Janey.

I hoped they were okay. After all, this whole idea had been mine. If anything happened to them, I could never forgive myself.

But I would have to deal with the bulldozer first, and that wasn't something I was looking forward to.

It charged toward me like an iron rhinoceros. Its front blade was raised off the ground, and I could see the big steel treads on either side of the machine tearing up the earth.

Battling the dozer would be impossible. It was far too big and powerful for Mr. Miller's tractor. I would have to deal with it in some other way.

I waited until the last possible second, and then I gunned the motor. The Miller's tractor shot forward and I turned the wheel, coming back up around and behind the dozer. It had missed me, and now it slowed and began to turn.

However, I found it easy to outmaneuver the beast, now that I didn't have to run from it. The dozer was huge, and its movements were slow. I was able to circle the machine like an excited puppy.

The dozer, unable to get at me, seemed to get angry. Thick, black exhaust spewed from its stack. The engine snarled like a lion. It raised and lowered its silvery blade wielding it like a sword, swinging it about like it was a weapon.

And it *was*. The blade *was* a weapon. In fact, the entire dozer was a weapon. All of the tractors and equipment that had come alive . . . they were weapons, too.

And that's when I suddenly had a daring plan.

*Weapons can be turned against themselves*, I thought, and as I circled the bulldozer and dashed out of its way, I had an idea.

One that just might work.

I glanced back at my house and caught a glimpse of John and Janey in the living room window. They were okay, after all. That was one less thing I had to worry about.

Because I needed to concentrate. If my plan was going to work, I couldn't screw up. Not one bit.

I whirled Mr. Miller's tractor next to one of the huge steel tracks that served as the tractors way of motion. I looked over at the empty seat, took a deep breath . . . and jumped onto the dozer.

# 33

My plan was this: get onto the bulldozer and pull the battery cable. If I could do that, I could stop the beast. Maybe not permanently, but it had worked before on the other tractors. When I had pulled the battery cables on the other tractors, they had stopped running right away.

As soon as I leapt onto the dozer, the thing went bananas. I mean complete, total, all-out *bananas*.

It started whirling and spinning around in a frenzy, changing directions every few seconds. It rocked forward and backward. Its motor revved and raced. I felt like I was riding a bull!

And I was! I was riding a bull . . . *dozer!*

I positioned myself on the seat in the cab, but it

was difficult to stay in one place. The dozer had gone berserk, and I was being tossed about like a leaf in a windstorm. If it kept up like this, there was no way I would be able to reach the battery cables.

The yellow bulldozer whirled, and I caught a glimpse of John and Janey through the living room window. They both had an expression of horror on their faces, like they were watching a scary movie.

The problem was, of course, what they were watching wasn't just a terrifying scene from a television show or a movie . . . it was very, very real.

I grabbed the steering levers for support. On this particular piece of machinery there was no steering wheel, but, rather, two levers used to control it.

There was no response at all. I had never used one of these huge contraptions before, and I'm sure that if Dad came home right now and saw me on the bulldozer, I'd be grounded for life. Maybe longer.

By holding the levers and sitting in the seat, I was able to steady myself. Again, I caught a glimpse of John and Janey looking at me through the window. Their faces were pressed against the glass, and both of them looked horrified.

Then the dozer suddenly careened around, snapping my head in another direction. The turn was so sudden, so violent, that it threw me to the floor of the cabin. I felt a sharp pain in my arm as I banged against something hard. It hurt bad, but at least it wasn't broken or anything.

It was then that I saw the battery cables. They were ahead of the small cab. The red and black cables looped out of the motor housing and wrapped back inside of it.

Another twist of the furious dozer sent me sprawling in the other direction, and I was almost tossed from the cab.

This wasn't going to work. I thought that if I could have reached the battery cables from the cab, I could stop the angry machine.

But it was all I could do to keep from falling off. If I tried to climb forward and reach the cables, I would be thrown from the dozer for sure . . . and then I wouldn't have a chance. Right now, the best thing I could do was hang on.

But I couldn't hang on forever. The dozer was churning and spinning, and I knew it would stop at nothing to throw me off. I felt like a bronco rider in a rampaging metal rodeo.

And then:

Disaster struck.

The dozer suddenly lurched to the side, slowed, then turned so violently I was thrown right out the

157

side of the cab and into the air.

*I was falling!*

Somehow, I missed landing on the churning metal tracking, and I hit the ground in a heap. The impact knocked the wind from me, and I gasped for air.

I rolled over and was about to get up and run, but it was already too late. The dozer had wheeled around, and its enormous metal blade was poised right above me.

Right then and there, I knew that I was done for. So far, I had been really lucky. We all had been.

But not any more. My luck had run out.

And when the giant blade began to come down, there was nothing I could do.

# 34

I snapped sideways, already knowing that it was probably too late. I didn't think I'd be able to get out of the way of the massive iron blade.

But the blade didn't come down all the way. It lowered only a little bit, then stopped. There was a grinding noise, and the blade came to a halt.

*The blade was stuck! It jammed and froze in place!* I could hear the hydraulic cylinder groaning, as it tried to un-jam itself.

I couldn't believe my luck, and I leapt to my feet and began running to the house. Several other tractors took chase, but they were too far away to get to me in time.

I bounded across the porch. John had opened

the front door for me, and I ran inside, breathless.

"Man, we thought you were history!" he exclaimed.

"The dozer's blade stuck," I said, gasping for air. "I can't believe my luck!"

I turned and looked outside.

Near the barn, the big yellow dozer had finally succeeded in getting its blade lowered to the ground. It was pushing dirt around like crazy, and thick, oily smoke was pouring from the exhaust stack.

"You sure made him mad," Janey said, bobbing her head up and down.

"He's mad all right," I replied. "They're all mad. This whole thing is mad. It's crazy."

There was a crash at the other end of the house. Windows rattled and pictures on the walls trembled. The floor beneath our feet shook.

"They're attacking again!" John shouted.

I began to realize that there was no way out of this. Our situation was, for the most part, hopeless. We were surrounded by a dozen pieces of heavy farming and construction equipment. For whatever reason, they had come alive . . . all by themselves. They were vicious, mean, and nasty.

And they weren't going to let us escape.

Not now. Not when they had us trapped.

I ran to the back door. A red International Harvester with yellow stripes patrolled the yard like a sentry, moving back and forth. A big yellow Caterpillar with huge black letters was digging holes with its gigantic bucket.

And I felt very, very sad. Before, I was simply afraid. I was afraid of the tractors and what they could do.

Now, after realizing that there was no escape, my fear turned to sadness and sorrow. We had no options but to wait it out. We would wait it out in the basement, but soon, the house would come crashing down on us.

I knew it would. The tractors and heavy machinery could demolish our home easily. We were three kids, and we were in way over our heads.

Outside, I watched the giant Caterpillar continue its laborious digging.

Suddenly, it stopped.

The red International Harvester tractor froze.

The roaring of engines ceased. Oh, the equipment was still running, but the engines weren't racing like they had been. Now, the noise from the machines had lowered to a steady hum.

I walked back to the front of the house where John and Janey stood. They, too, were watching the motionless tractors in the front yard and the pasture.

None were moving. For the first time that afternoon, the tractors weren't destroying everything in sight.

"What's going on?" John asked. "Are they out of fuel?"

I shook my head. "No," I replied. "They're still running."

And then:

One by one, they began to move.

Slowly.

Methodically.

Mechanically.

Slowly . . . so very slowly . . . they began to turn. They were turning . . .away from the house!

It was as if they were all looking in the same direction. They were all looking down the road, as if they were expecting something. Like something was coming.

And then—I could *feel* it.

A rumbling beneath my feet. A gentle trembling that was growing stronger.

Something *was* coming.

I could feel it. John and Janey could feel it.

The tractors and heavy machinery in the yard remained frozen in place. They were still running, but all of the equipment, all of the tractors and dozers and loaders, were pointed toward the crest of a hill in the road.

And I was hopeful.

*Maybe we're being rescued*, I thought. *Maybe someone is coming to save us.*

My hope suddenly went down the drain. When I saw what was coming over the hill and down the road, I knew that it was over . . . for *all* of us.

# 35

A monstrous, yellow front end loader was coming.

And it was nothing less than a beast.

It was the biggest, meanest, nastiest, most gargantuan piece of machinery I had ever seen. Its tires were three time taller than I was. It had a front bucket that could scoop up a truck, and a rear bucket that was just as big. It would easily turn our home into toothpicks.

And it was coming down the road, straight for us.

We were too shocked to move. Janey started to sniffle, and then she started to cry. John held her hand.

All we could do was wait. We could only watch

and wait as the massive loader came closer and closer, directly toward our home.

Suddenly, the other tractors and equipment around the farm began to move. But they weren't coming toward the house . . . they were moving toward the giant loader!

A small green and yellow tractor attacked the enormous yellow beast . . . but the loader squished the tiny tractor with a single swipe of its huge front bucket. Metal snapped and crunched. The giant yellow monster didn't even have to slow down.

Another piece of machinery attacked. It was an Agco Allis tractor, and it tried to ram the yellow loader head-on. It was quickly rolled over and crushed.

*"What's going on here?!?!"* John asked.

I said nothing. All I could do was shake my head.

And the mammoth metal monstrosity kept coming toward the house, faster and faster. Raging black smoke pumped out of its exhaust stack. Its motor sounded like some deranged, snarling animal.

"Let's get out of here!" John cried. He began to run to the back of the house, but I grabbed his arm.

"Hang on a minute!" I exclaimed. "Something is going on here!"

"Yeah! We're about to be squished!" John replied.

"No," I said. "Look!"

As we watched, more and more of our farm machinery attacked that giant yellow monster. They were all smashed, crunched and ground down to nothing more than useless scrap metal.

*"Someone is driving it!"* John suddenly shouted.

*He was right! I could see the shape of someone inside the cab on top of the huge loader!*

The machine lurched to the left and ran over a small garden tractor that had tried to attack. Then it pulled into our driveway and barreled toward us.

I could clearly see someone sitting up in the cab. As the yellow beast drew closer, it slowed, finally stopping in front of our house. Most of the other tractors and heavy equipment had been demolished, hopelessly hobbled.

I can't begin to tell you how relieved we were. We had thought that all hope had been lost.

But this giant front end loader . . . and the guy driving it . . . had saved the day!

We ran to the front door. The man on the loader was climbing out of the cab. It was like he was coming down from a three-story house!

We burst out the front door, across the porch, and over the lawn.

"Man, are we glad you're here!" I shouted to the

man.

He was wearing blue jeans and a red T-shirt, and he scrambled to the ground and walked toward us.

"I'm sorry I didn't believe you the first time," he said, shaking his head.

*Huh?* I thought. *What was he talking about?*

"What do you mean?" I asked.

"On the radio," he replied. "I was over on the freeway when you called for help. I thought you were fooling around."

*The guy I talked to on the radio! It was him!*

"But . . . if you didn't believe us, then why did you come to help?" John asked.

"When you were speaking, I heard an awful noise. Then the radio went dead. I figured that something really *was* wrong."

"That was when the barn crashed down!" I exclaimed. "When I was talking to you, the tractors attacked the barn. It came crashing down to the ground!"

"I was driving a semi truck with this here loader on the trailer," he continued, pointing over his shoulder at the yellow machine. "When I heard that crash, I figured you weren't pulling my leg, after all. I stopped my truck, backed this thing off the trailer, and drove it here. I wish I could have made it here sooner."

"You saved us from—"

There was a sudden rumbling behind us. I stopped speaking, and we all gazed in the direction of the noise.

A car was coming.

No, not just a car.

*It was Mom and Dad!*

# 36

As you can imagine, Mom and Dad both freaked. The farm looked like a junkyard, and when Dad got out of the car, he couldn't even speak.

"What . . . how . . . when?" he stammered.

I got busy explaining, and let me tell you—it was a chore to convince him of the truth! Here I was telling my own dad that tractors had come to life by themselves. They had attacked everything in sight, including us!

At first, there was no way he was going to believe me. But the guy who drove the giant loader came to our rescue again.

"It's true," he explained to Dad. "When I came over that ridge, I saw all these tractors driving all by themselves. It was crazy. They attacked my loader, but no one was driving them."

In the end, Dad and Mom finally believed us. No one could figure out how the machines had come to life.

Until a car came screaming down the road. It whipped into our driveway and grinded to a halt on the dirt. A man burst out the door.

"Oh no!" he cried, as he looked around. "Oh no!"

*It was the man that had sold Dad the experimental fuel!*

"I tried to get here before it was too late!" he said sadly. "Was anyone hurt?"

We shook our heads, but Janey spoke up.

"I scraped my arm," she said, showing her elbow.

"None of us was really hurt," I said. "But . . . how did all of this happen?"

"The experimental fuel," he explained. "I've been working on it for years. It's a special 'computer' fuel, that actually works like a computer."

"Like . . . it has a brain?" John asked.

"Well, sort of," the man said. "I programmed it to help engines run better and longer. I didn't plan on something like this happening. You're not the only folks who have had problems. But, thankfully, no one has been hurt."

What a strange day this had turned out to be.

John and Janey's Mom and Dad had to come and pick them up early, since we couldn't stay in the house. A lot of damage had been done, and Dad said that we would have to move into a hotel until the repairs were finished.

But I was glad it was all over. What had happened had been worse than any nightmare that I've ever had. All around the farm, broken and crushed equipment was strewn about. The people from the television station even came out and did a report about what had happened. I sure was glad that there were no more machines or equipment coming to life.

I was about to find out that I was wrong.

That evening, when I was packing up some clothes to take to the hotel, I was loading a bag into our car. Mom and Dad were in the house packing. There was no one in the car.

Suddenly, the car engine roared to life! The keys weren't even in the ignition, but the motor had started . . . *all by itself!*

# 37

I screamed and fled. The car continued to idle under its own power, despite the fact that no one had started it and there were no keys in the ignition.

I ran toward the house. Mom was already at the door. She had a frantic look on her face.

"What?!?!?" she asked as I reached the porch.

I turned and pointed. "The car!" I yelled. "It started all by itself!"

Mom looked at the car, and Dad came to the front door. "What's the matter?" he asked.

"The car!" I explained. "It's running! Look! It started all by itself!"

Dad looked at the car, then held out his hand, displaying a small, matchbook-sized object. It was black and had several buttons on it.

"It's a remote starter," he said. "We bought it earlier today. You can start your car with it, and not use the keys."

I let out a sigh of relief. "Wow, that really spooked me," I said.

"Sorry about that," Dad said. "I guess, with everything that happened today, I shouldn't have done that. Are you all packed?"

"Yeah," I said, nodding.

"Okay. We've got a few more things to get and we'll be ready to go."

■ ■ ■

We settled into a hotel that wasn't far away. It had a pool and a hot tub and a game room. Dad said that we'd have to live there until the house was fixed up.

Which wasn't too bad. The hired hands would still go to work at our ranch with Dad, but they'd be doing a lot of picking up and a lot of repair work. Most of the tractors were so badly damaged that they had to be scrapped.

And I had to work, too. Dad and Mom and I drove out to the house every day to help clean things up. Plus, all of the animals had to be looked after. It was hard work, especially under the blazing summer sun. But in the evening we would drive back to the hotel, and I got to swim in the pool and play in the game room.

One evening, after a long day working, I was swimming in the pool when two kids came in. A boy and a girl, each about my age, plopped into the water. After a few minutes, we began talking. The girl was Alyssa, the boy was Ryan. They were from Illinois, and they were visiting Texas for a vacation. Alyssa was really talkative, but Ryan was kind of shy.

"Don't mind my brother," Alyssa said. "He's usually a chatterbox, and he talks all the time. But he's still a little freaked out."

"Freaked out?" I asked. "Why?"

Alyssa started to swim away. "I don't even want to get into it," she said. "You wouldn't believe me, anyway."

"Yes, I will," I said, swimming after her. "What happened?"

She stopped at the edge of the pool where a white towel was waiting for her. She picked it up and dried her face. Her brother climbed out of the pool and went into the game room.

"No one has believed us so far, so why should I tell you?" she asked.

And so, I told her all about the tractors that had come to life. I told her what had happened to our house and the farm. She listened, her eyes wide.

"That's pretty weird," she said. "That's as weird as the things that happened to Ryan and I."

"What?" I pressed. "What happened to you guys?"

Alyssa took a breath, and looked around. It was like she was making sure that no one else was listening.

"Iguanas," she said, almost under her breath.

"Huh?" I said.

"Iguanas," she repeated.

"Like . . . lizards?" I asked.

Alyssa nodded. "Exactly," she said.

"What's so bad about iguanas?" I asked. "Lots of people have them as pets."

She shook her head. "It's not really the iguanas," she replied. "It's what happened to them."

I still couldn't figure out what the big deal was. A friend of mine has an iguana as a pet, and it's pretty cool. It's about as long as my arm. He feeds it vegetables and sometimes fruit.

"What happened to them?" I asked. "What's so bad about iguanas?"

Again, Alyssa looked around to make sure no one

else was listening.

"These iguanas," she said softly, "aren't like any other iguanas you've ever seen." Her eyes lit up. "In fact, sometimes you can't see them at all."

*Huh? What was she talking about?*

"You can't see them?" I asked. This was pretty confusing.

"That's right," she replied. "These iguanas are *invisible.*"

And for the next hour, I sat at the edge of the pool while she told me what had happened to her.

I had thought that what had happened with the tractors would be the strangest thing I'd ever heard.

Not anymore. What Alyssa told me gives me chills to this very day . . . .

*next in the*

# AMERICAN CHILLERS

*series:*

# #6:

# INVISIBLE

# IGUANAS

# OF

# ILLINOIS

*go to the next page to read a few spine-
chilling chapters . . . if you dare!*

# 1

When someone tells you a story, they usually start at the beginning.

And that's where I'm going to start. You have to know a couple of things before you can try to understand what has happened and why. And I will say this much:

What you are about to read is going to be pretty frightening at times. Not always, because there were some funny things that happened, too. But, for the most part, what my brother and I went through was pretty scary.

My name is Alyssa Barryton, and I'm eleven.

I have a brother named Ryan. He's ten, but sometimes he doesn't act like it. Sometimes he acts like he's two!

We live in Springfield, Illinois. You've probably heard or read about our state, because Illinois is called the 'Land of Lincoln'. Abraham Lincoln called Illinois his home for over 30 years. In fact, if you ever come to Springfield, you can visit Abraham Lincoln's home. You'll see lots of really cool historical places.

But I doubt you'll see what I saw last year. Matter of fact, even I probably won't see it again.

I was walking to a friend's house after school. A group of us were going to meet and go for a bike ride along Lost Bridge Trail. It's a really cool paved path that's about five miles long. A lot of people jog, walk, and even rollerblade along the trail.

I stopped at a market that sells fresh fruits and vegetables and bought a small bag of radishes. That's right—radishes. I *love* radishes. I eat them raw, right out of the bag. I eat them the way most people eat candy.

I had just walked out the door and was

opening the bag when I heard a noise from the alley next to the store. It was a swishing sound.

I turned and looked down the alley. The only things I saw were a few garbage cans and a single parked car.

I didn't think anything of it, and I started to turn my head away.

And then:

*I saw something.*

Out of the corner of my eye, something had moved. Something had darted behind the garbage cans.

I stopped walking and scanned the alley to see what was there. The sun was shining, and the day was warm. It was the middle of June, and the summers can be pretty hot here in Springfield.

But I didn't see anything.

I pulled out a radish and popped it into my mouth.

*Just an old alley cat,* I thought. I reached into the bag and pulled out another red radish.

I turned and started to walk away, but I heard the noise again. It was the sound of something moving, shuffling across papers or leaves.

Once more, I glanced down the alley.
I stopped chewing my gum.
I almost dropped my bottle of juice.
What I saw wasn't a cat.
Or a dog.
Or a pigeon or a rabbit.
*It was a tiny creature from outer space!*

# 2

I blinked my eyes, and I realized what I was seeing wasn't a creature from outer space.

It was an *iguana!*

A lizard . . . a real, live iguana . . . was staring back at me! He was about a foot tall and three feet long, and he was standing next to a garbage can! I could see his beady black eyes watching me.

Now, you have to understand something: Iguanas don't live in Illinois.

*Period.*

Oh, some people have them as pets, of course. And I saw a real big one at the Chicago Zoo.

But iguanas don't live in the wild . . . not in Illinois, they don't.

Which would explain why I thought that it was a creature from outer space!

The lizard turned his head. It was a bright green color, and it stood about as tall as a cat, only it was longer. And it had scales that began at the back of its head and went down the middle of its back. Its claws were long and sharp, like hooked nails.

Now, I didn't know anything about iguanas. I didn't know if they were vicious, or if they bit people. Who knows? Maybe they even *eat* people!

But I didn't think so. I don't think people would have them as pets if they ate humans.

I wanted to get closer so I could see the creature better. I took a real slow step, and then another.

The iguana didn't move. It just stood there on its four legs, flashing his dark eyes at me.

Slowly, very slowly, I made my way down the alley.

*Closer* . . . .

*Closer . . . .*

The iguana didn't move much. He turned his head a couple of times, but he continued eyeing me cautiously.

And it was really cool looking! I hadn't seen many iguanas before, except the one in the zoo. Now I was only a few feet away from one!

I stopped and held my breath. I kept expecting the creature to suddenly run off, to dart behind the garbage cans.

But it didn't. It just stared at me.

I knelt down very slowly.

"Hey, buddy," I said sweetly. "Whatcha doin'?"

The lizard remained where he was.

"You're kind of cute," I said.

The iguana responded by opening his mouth.

*Uh-oh,* I thought. *Maybe he's getting mad.*

I had just started to stand back up when the lizard reared back, opened his mouth even wider, and charged!

*The iguana was attacking!*

# 3

I didn't know what to do!  I had never been
attacked by an iguana before!

   And besides . . .  I didn't have time to do
anything, anyway.  In less than a second the
iguana had reached me.

   I twisted to get out of the way, and in my
haste, I slipped, dropped my bag of
radishes—and fell.

   I tumbled onto my back, and the lizard seized
the opportunity.  Before I could do anything, it
had scrambled up my leg and onto my stomach.

   I was sure that this was the end for me.

Maybe iguanas eat people, after all.

I tried to scream, but no sound came out. My eyes were popping out of my head as the iguana came to a rest on my chest. Its mouth was closed, but its black eyes were staring right into mine.

This was a nightmare. It had to be. I kept telling myself to wake up, to shake the dream away, but I couldn't.

And I could feel the lizard's heartbeat. Its belly was pressed against my shirt, and I could actually feel its pounding heart going a mile a minute.

I took long, slow breaths. I didn't want the heaving of my chest to disturb the beast. It might make him even more mad.

The lizard turned his head, looking around. It blinked a few times.

"*Help,*" I managed to say. But it was more of a squeak than anything, and besides . . . there was no one around to help, anyway.

"*You're . . . you're not going to hurt me, are you?*" I said to the lizard. I know that it probably was a silly thing to do, but hey . . . I didn't know what else to do.

When he heard my voice, he cocked his head to the side like a dog listening to a high-pitched sound.

*Maybe it's friendly*, I thought. *Maybe it's not mean, after all.*

I was wrong.

The iguana suddenly turned its head and stared directly into my eyes. It opened its mouth, and I could see rows and rows of teeth. They were really tiny — not like fangs or anything — but I knew that they were probably razor sharp.

And without warning, the vicious reptile lurched forward, mouth open and teeth bared. I could only watch in horror as the horrible lizard attacked, searching for the soft, tender flesh of my neck!

# 4

Talk about being freaked!

I was frozen in fear and I closed my eyes, waiting for the razor-sharp teeth to sink into my neck—

*But the bite never came!*

I had my eyes closed tightly, and I felt the iguana scramble up over my shoulder.

Then I heard a crunch, and I just knew that it was biting my ear.

And I didn't feel any pain!

Then I heard another crunch. And another. And then a chewing sound.

I opened my eyes and slowly turned my head. *The iguana was eating a radish!* Its jaw was going up and down, up and down, and it looked as happy as a clam!

Suddenly, I felt very foolish. I had been frightened by the creature . . . and all he wanted was a radish!

I scooched sideways and moved away from the lizard. It paid no attention. It just kept chewing on the radish.

"Hey," I said, "you're kinda cool." The iguana stretched out its neck and snared another radish.

Watching the creature and being so close at the same time was really awesome. Its skin was the color of summer leaves, and its eyes were the blackest of black.

And I began to wonder where it had come from. I didn't know a lot about iguanas, but I knew enough to know that they don't live in Illinois unless they're someone's pet.

*That's it,* I thought. *This must be someone's pet. I'll bet it's friendly.*

It was risky, but I reached over and picked up

the bag of radishes. The iguana was busy chewing on one, and it didn't do anything but continue chewing.

When it was done, I reached into the bag and pulled out another radish. I held it out.

*The lizard took it! It ate right out of my hand!*

This was really, really cool.

While he was chewing on the radish, I reached out again, very slowly, and touched the back of its head. The lizard instantly stopped chewing.

The iguana liked it! It liked being petted!

Then I began to wonder: Just who does this creature belong to? Someone must be looking for it. We have a black cat named Spooky, and if we ever lost him, we'd be looking all over the place for him. I was sure someone would be searching for their pet iguana.

Gently . . . ever so gently . . . I picked up the creature and cradled it in my arms like a baby. It didn't seem to mind at all.

I looked around to see if I could see anyone that seemed to be looking for something.

Nope.

Then, I walked up the alley and looked

around. Cars sped by on the street, and there were a few people out walking around, but no one seemed to be looking for an iguana.

I walked back into the market and asked a woman at the service counter if anyone was missing an iguana.

That was a big mistake.

Now, I kind of figured that if anyone saw me carrying around an iguana in the store, they'd probably look twice. After all, it's not every day that you see a girl carrying a lizard around.

But when the woman at the service counter saw the lizard in my arms, she flipped out!

"Get that thing out of here this instant young lady!" she ordered. "This place sells food! We can't have ugly green snakes in here!"

"It's not a snake," I replied. "It's an iguana."

"I don't care!" she snapped. "Get that disgusting creature out of the store!"

So, I had no choice but to take the lizard home. I figured that I could maybe make some signs and put them up around the neighborhood. Somewhere, someone was looking for their pet iguana. I just knew it.

Thankfully, Mom and Dad said that I could keep the reptile . . . but only until I found its owner. My brother Ryan thought that it was really cool, but he was a little afraid of it.

I called the pet store to find out how to take care of the iguana. Let me tell you . . . caring for an iguana is *nothing* like caring for a dog or a cat! An iguana takes a lot of hard work. I learned that they could be really great pets, but I also found out that they needed a lot of attention.

And that's how I came to have Iggy. Yep. You guessed it. I never found the owner. The man at the pet store said that some people don't realize how much work an iguana can be, and they just let them go to fend for themselves.

How horrible! Who would do such a thing?!?!

But if I thought *that* was horrible, it was *nothing* compared to the things that were about to happen.

And I will say this:

Prepare yourself. Because what was about to happen wasn't just *scary*.

It was *horrifying* . . . with a capital 'H'.

**Also by Johnathan Rand:**

# GHOST IN THE GRAVEYARD

# About the author

Johnathan Rand is the author of the best-selling **'Chillers'** series, now with over 1,500,000 copies in print. In addition to the **'Chillers'** series, Rand is also the author of the 'Adventure Club' series, including **'Ghost in the Graveyard' and 'Ghost in the Grand'**, two collections of thrilling, original short stories. When Mr. Rand and his wife are not traveling to schools and book signings, they live in a small town in northern lower Michigan with their three dogs, Abby, Salty, and Lily Munster. He still writes all of his books in the wee hours of the morning, and still submits all manuscripts by mail. He is currently working on more **'American Chillers'** and a new series of audiobooks called **'Creepy Campfire Chillers'**. His popular website features hundreds of photographs, stories, and art work. Visit:

## www.americanchillers.com

# FUN
# FACTS ABOUT TEXAS:

State Capitol: Austin

Became a state in 1845

State Motto: Friendship

State Bird: Mockingbird

State Insect: Monarch Butterfly

State Tree: Pecan

State Fish: Guadalupe Bass

State Flower: Bluebonnet

State Nickname: The Lone Star State

The total area of Texas is 261,914 square miles!

# INTERESTING TEXAS TRIVIA!

☞ **Texas is the country's biggest producer of oil, cattle, sheep, minerals and cotton.**

☞ **Texas is the second largest state in the US.**

☞ **The first Europeans were Spanish explorers, such as Coronado, who traveled the region in the 16th and 17th centuries.**

☞ **According to the *Guiness Book of World Records*, there are 20 million bats in Bracken Cave, located in San Antonio, Texas!**

☞ **The Whooping Crane is Texas' tallest bird at five feet tall. It has an enormous wingspan of seven and one half feet!**

Join the official

# AMERICAN CHILLERS

## FAN CLUB!

Visit www.americanchillers.com for details!

About the cover art: This unique cover was designed and created by Michigan artists Darrin Brege and Mark Thompson.

**Darrin Brege** works as an animator by day, and is now applying his talents on the internet, creating various web sites and flash animations. He attended animation school in southern California in the early nineties, and over the years has created original characters and animations for Warner Bros (Space Jam), for Hasbro (Tonka Joe Multimedia line), Universal Pictures (Bullwinkle and Fractured Fairy Tales CD Roms), and Disney. Besides art, he and his wife Karen are improv performers featured weekly at Mark Ridley's Comedy Castle over the last eight years. Improvisational comedy has provided the groundwork for a successful voice over career as well. Darrin has dozens of characters and impersonations in his portfolio. Darrin and Karen have a son named Mick.

**Mark Thompson** has been a professional illustrator for 25 years. He has applied his talents with toy companies Hasbro and Mattel, along with creating art for automobile companies. His work has been seen from San Diego Seaworld to Kmart stores, as well as the Detroit Tigers and the renowned 'Screams' ice-cream parlor in Hell, Michigan. Mark currently is designing holiday crafts for a local company, as well as doing website design and digital art from his home studio. He loves sci-fi and monster art, and also collects comics for a hobby. He has two boys of his own, and they're BIG Chiller Fans!